Slave . . .

"You like being a slave?" he asked.

Slave? Me? I said nothing. He was watching me, so I kept my face from showing anything. I couldn't stop my eyes though. They said things. I couldn't help it. And he saw, too.

"What's wrong?" he asked.

"I'm not a slave," I said.

He laughed then. He threw his head back. "What are you, then?"

"I'm Harriet Hemings." My eyes were getting tears in them.

"Yes, you're Harriet Hemings." But he didn't say it unkindly. He is most kind, most attentive. "Sally Hemings' little girl. Tutored. Dressed most properly. Does a little work in the weaver's cottage every morning. Lives upstairs on the third floor. Like a household pet. . . ."

Other Point paperbacks
you will enjoy:

This Strange New Feeling
by Julius Lester

My Brother Sam Is Dead
by James Lincoln Collier and Christopher Collier

A Band of Angels
by Julian Thompson

Fallen Angels
by Walter Dean Myers

Dawn Rider
by Jan Hudson

Wolf by the Ears

Ann Rinaldi

SCHOLASTIC INC.
New York Toronto London Auckland Sydney

ISBN 0-590-43412-8

12   0 1 2/0

Printed in the U.S.A.   01

For Michael Scott,
my first grandchild,
who is always welcome to interrupt my writing
and give me back my perspective.

Acknowledgments

No historical novelist works alone. So I owe a debt of gratitude to the people who helped me in my research for this book, especially the writers of the many books on Thomas Jefferson.

Special thanks go to Lucia C. Stanton, Director of Research at Monticello, for supplying me with the dates when Harriet and Beverly ran away.

If appreciation goes to anyone, it goes to Joanna Cole, my agent, who believed in this book from the beginning, and to Regina Griffin, my editor at Scholastic, who fought to make this vision of mine a reality.

My heartfelt appreciation goes to my family, who gave me the "space" to write, especially my husband, Ron, who never begrudged me my work. And to our daughter, who, both by her wedding to Scott Loureiro, and by presenting us with our first grandson, Michael, just as the book was completed, brought her own particular brand of brightness into my life.

No historical novel of mine would ever have been undertaken had I not been influenced by my son, Ron, who started a love affair with American history at age fourteen. Ron addicted me to the subject. It is a debt I can never repay. Not to mention the use I had of his very extensive library of American and U.S. military history.

As Ron was growing up, his heroes were George Washington, Thomas Jefferson, John Adams, Benjamin Franklin, Alexander Hamilton, and all those other wonderful people fate conspired to bring together to form our country. These people helped form Ron's foundation for life, which, when tested, held strong. Ron has gone into law enforcement and is now with the Delaware State Police.

It is for this reason that I write historical fiction for young people. If I can "turn them on" to our country's past, and seize their imaginations as Ron's was seized, then I may succeed in doing something really worthwhile.

Ann Rinaldi

Author's Note

Years ago I read a book on Thomas Jefferson's private life, which was only one of many written on the principal author of the Declaration of Independence. This book, *Thomas Jefferson: An Intimate History* (W.W. Norton, 1974), by Fawn M. Brodie, a professor of history at UCLA, suggested that Jefferson, widowed at thirty-nine, had children with Sally Hemings, one of his slaves.

Brodie's book and articles affected me deeply. I could not bear to think, as Brodie had written, that these children, who might have been the unacknowledged offspring of so great a man, had to wait to be freed by him, or, as in the case of Tom Hemings and his brother Beverly, had to run away. And then there was Harriet, who was reportedly given her freedom at age twenty-one and with Thomas Jefferson's blessing, provided with money and transportation in order to make her own way in the world. How terrible! Over the years this thought stayed in back of my mind and came to surface again, years later, after I had successfully raised my own children and wanted to do an historical novel about alienation.

The theme of alienation has always intrigued me. The dictionary defines "alienate" as 1. "to make unfriendly or withdrawn," and 2. "to cause transference of affection."

My own mother had died when I was born. I never knew her family or even saw a picture of her until I was married. So there was always a part of me I could not acknowledge, a part of me I yearned to understand.

I felt I understood the confusion that comes from being denied one's rightful heritage. And, when looking for a real figure in American history to write about in connection with alienation, I recalled Harriet Hemings and her brothers.

So I did more research and, using every fact I could find about Monticello, Thomas Jefferson, and the Hemings family, I put together my story.

First, it is important for the reader to know that I did not write this book to "put down" Thomas Jefferson. I greatly admire the man. Along with George Washington, Light Horse Harry Lee, General Anthony Wayne, Benjamin Franklin, and all those others whose brilliance and courage conspired at the right time to start our new nation, he has always been one of my heroes.

My research, however, only told me bits and pieces about Harriet Hemings. And so, within a framework of fact, I invented my own Harriet. I decided that "my Harriet" would not want to leave Monticello when she came of age, although, like all of Sally Hemings' children, she was to be given her freedom at age twenty-one.

I decided that my story would be about what convinced her to understand how important freedom was and to sacrifice everything she knew, everything that was reassuring and comforting, to finally take it.

Second, it is important that the reader know that I have portrayed Jefferson's character as faithfully as I found it to be, after intensive study. Many of his quotes and sentiments are taken from his letters. I do not wish to distort or improve upon American history. I wish to interpret it through my fiction, to make it more interesting so my readers, once their interest is quickened, will pursue it further.

Third, and most important — I do not claim to know what it felt like to be a slave, to be half black or three-quarters white. But I do know how it feels to be alienated, to wonder about part of one's background, and to be unable to get over the idea that one never quite belongs. These feelings are human, not exclusively belonging to blacks, whites, or anyone else. And if my book pleases, then it crosses all those artificial barriers we put up to distance us from one another and speaks to the soul in my readers. Which is what good writing is supposed to be all about.

Ann Rinaldi

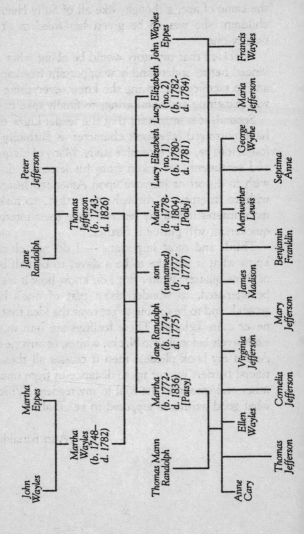

The Jefferson Family

The Hemings Family

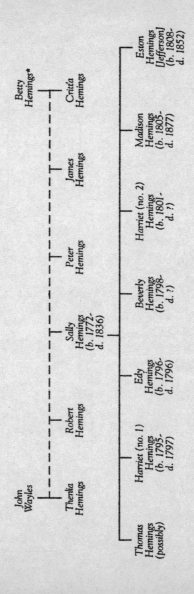

John Wayles — Thenia Hemings

Betty Hemings* — Critta Hemings

Thomas Hemings (possibly)

Harriet (no. 1) Hemings (b. 1795- d. 1797)

Robert Hemings

Edy Hemings (b. 1796- d. 1796)

Sally Hemings (b. 1772- d. 1836)

Beverly Hemings (b. 1798- d. ?)

Peter Hemings

Harriet (no. 2) Hemings (b. 1801- d. ?)

James Hemings

Madison Hemings (b. 1805- d. 1877)

Eston Hemings [Jefferson] (b. 1808- d. 1852)

*These are her children with John Wayles only.

Wolf by the Ears

". . . Gradually, with due sacrifices, a general emancipation and expatriation could be effected. But as it is, we have the wolf by the ears, and we can neither hold him, nor safely let him go. Justice is in one scale, and self-preservation the other."

— *Thomas Jefferson*

December 1819

Only twice in all my years on this place have I ever been inside the master's private quarters. No one is allowed in there. Only my mama. And that's because she is the mistress of his wardrobe.

He calls those rooms his sanctum sanctorum.

The two instances I was inside them I shall remember always. For they marked a change in my life each time.

The first occasion was a snowy afternoon this December. Early darkness that accompanies a snowstorm had descended on the whole place. And though it was only three in the afternoon, candles were already lighted in the lower part of the house. And everyone, nigra servants and white folk alike, was greatly agitated by the snow. Outside the windows, in whatever direction we looked, flakes were swirling down. It was the first real snowfall of the season, and the world was getting closed off quickly.

My younger brothers, Madison and Eston, had been assigned by Martha Randolph, who is the master's daughter, to sweep off the east portico. But all we could hear from out there were shrieks and shouts. Which told us they were engaged in activities other than sweeping.

Several times Martha got up from her sewing and wrapped a shawl around herself and took her aching body, as she called it, to the doors of the east portico to scold my brothers. And her own parcel of ruffians who were with them. That is, her Benjamin Franklin, who is twelve, her Meriwether Lewis, who is ten, and little Georgie Wythe, who is two. She has eleven children all together.

My brothers, Madison and Eston, are fifteen and thirteen.

Every time she went out to scold, a blast of cold wind came in. They would get quiet out there on the portico for a while. Mama and I had just come from upstairs. I usually work in the weaver's cottage, but we'd been dismissed early because of the weather, and I was helping Mama distribute woolen blankets to all the beds in the household.

Mama had her arms full of blankets, and the foolery outside commenced again. Mama suggested that Martha bring an end to it. And so Martha went out to take command. Which is what she is best at anyway.

It was then that Mama directed me to go into the dining room and fetch the tray of tea that was being

4

sent up on the dumbwaiter. And to follow her into the master's quarters.

"He's been writing all day," she said. "I'm afraid he'll take a chill."

I was so dumbstruck I could scarcely speak. My senses were in a fevered pitch because of the snow, and I'd been about to ask Mama if I could go outside, too. Why should Madison and Eston have all the merriment?

But being invited into the master's sanctum sanctorum was a much better arrangement.

When I saw the tray, I was surprised to see on it a caudle of warm broth mixed with wine. The steamy fragrance of it made me hungry. But such a mixture was for sick folk. I felt a stab of fear. Was the master sick?

"Be careful with that tray," Mama admonished. I followed her into the hall that led to the master's quarters. "You set it down where and when I tell you. And don't lollygag about after. Unless he speaks to you. Which he probably won't, because he hasn't spoken to anyone in almost twenty-four hours, since he started writing that fool autobiography of his."

"What's an autobiography, Mama?" I asked.

"It's a story a person writes about their own life."

"Will the master put you in it?"

But she did not answer. Burwell was coming out of the master's quarters. Burwell is his body servant. He shuffles now because he's so old. But he's the only one the master will tolerate fussing around in his quarters besides Mama.

Burwell tells Mama that he just stoked the fire. You want I should take in the tray, he asks her.

She says no. Harriet can do it. You have enough to do keeping his fire going. "If those boys of mine ever get the porticos swept off, they could bring in more wood so's you don't have to go out in the cold, Burwell," she tells him.

Seems your boys need fetching, Burwell says. You want I'll get them in, Sally.

Mama says please, yes. Before they come down with the pleurisy. Mama has herself a regular fixation about si kness. She's seen so much of it.

Now all this exchange was done in whispers, as befits the private quarters of the master. Burwell left then, and we went through another door. And there we were, in the master's bedroom.

I stopped dead in my tracks, rooted to the spot. I looked around. Lollygagging wasn't the word for it. My eyes were popping right out of my head.

"Stop staring!" Mama whispers. "Come along!"

I followed her. Just ahead was his bed. It's in an alcove. And it is hung with red brocade. And through the alcove I could see his cabinet room.

And there he sat, just like God on Judgment Day.

He was writing. And he did not look up. So I took a precious moment to look around. He was seated in his chaise lounge with the candles on the arms for illumination.

There was his polygraph. I'd heard about that. He had it made for copying his letters. He was forever writing letters.

On the window seat was his telescope. His surveying equipment stood in the doorway that led to the south piazza landing. I tried to fix everything in my head so I would always remember. Then Mama pointed, and I set down the tray.

Mama was pouring his tea. He put down his quill pen now, and he had the caudle in his hands. He was sipping it. Mama put a shawl around his shoulders. They had forgotten me. They were discussing the snow. So I took the occasion to let my eyes wander.

And there, above the master's bed, were the portholes in the wall.

There is my mama's room, I said to myself. I knew it as sure as I knew my own name. My brother Beverly told me she had a room up there. Of course, in the household it was forever unspoken.

My eyes had just gotten past those portholes to the skylight in the ceiling. Through it I could see the swirling snow. Then Mama nudged me.

You may go now, Harriet, she said.

But the master held up his hand. "Let her stay a moment," he said. "How are you, Harriet?"

Well, I remembered to curtsy. I may be flighty at times, like Mama says, but I do have manners.

"I'm tolerable, Master," I said.

He smiled, and I felt a sense of peace wash over me. He has those blue eyes, and there is all of the sky in them. When he gets angry, they are like the sky before a storm. I have seen him look at others that way. But never at me. Always when those eyes are directed at me, the sky is full of sunlight.

7

"Only tolerable?" he says. "And why? Haven't they allowed you to play in the snow with your brothers and my grandchildren?"

"I'm getting too old for that, Master," I said. I was very dignified saying it.

He laughed then. He set the caudle down. "Oh, I can see that, Harriet. You're growing like a jonquil flower. And Mr. Oglesby tells me you're doing well with your lessons."

"Thank you, Master," I said.

"He also reports that your penmanship is superior to your brothers'."

"I'm most gratified, Master," I said. "But Beverly is better at reading."

I pleasured him then. "Ah," he said. "Modesty does so become a young woman, Harriet. I am happy to see that quality in you. Yes, your brother is in my library all the time. I see you're looking at my papers. I'm attempting to write my autobiography."

"Will you put my mama in it?" I asked.

He only smiled. But now the eyes were sad. "Writing is a wonderful pastime, Harriet, after the occupations of the fields and garden. If we must be shut up, it eases the drudgery. I've been so busy all day I've scarcely noticed the weather."

"The top of the Blue Ridge is white with snow," I reported to him.

He smiled. "Ah, Harriet, thank you. I must enter that in my Farm Book." I knew about his Farm Book, of course, how he noted the date of the appearance of every vegetable and fruit, every blossom, every inch of snow, as well as his formulas for farming and his observations on creatures.

And because of this Farm Book we shared a secret, he and I. Every time I saw him, I tried to give him some observation of mine for his book. Always he said he would mark it down.

Now he did something that was not uncommon for him but that surprised me nevertheless. He reached amongst his papers and drew out a small, square leatherbound book. "Take this, Harriet," he said.

As I said, it was not uncommon for him to give me or my brothers small gifts when we visited with him. A phial of seeds, a bird's feather, a piece of fresh fruit or a small book. But now I just stared as he held the gift out to me. I looked at Mama, and she nodded yes. So I accepted it. Lovingly I smoothed my hands over the burnished leather cover.

"You notice the wonders of nature more than any child on this place," he said to me. "I like that. Write down what you see, what is important to you, whether it be the sound of a bird, the snow on the Blue Ridge, or the taste of your mama's salmagundi."

"Thank you, Master. I am most gratified."

He nodded. "Write down what you feel, Harriet. It eases the heart. You will discover that in your own good time. Writing cures the useless hours of their boredom."

And so it was that on a cold day in December, Thomas Jefferson, my master, gave me this journal to write in.

I, a nigra servant.

9

I mark here the word servant. And not slave. For no white person on this place calls us slaves. But that is what we be. All of us.

Yet I feel that I am more. I know I am more.

Otherwise he would not have given this book to me. Would he?

April 1820

So here I am, and it is four months since the master gave me this journal to write in, and only today, this fine day in April, have I started to write in it.

I am Harriet. I want to get that down plain. I am the third child of my mother, Sally Hemings. The third to live, I mark here. There was another Harriet before me, who was birthed in 1795. But she died at the age of two, of the pleurisy. My mama then had another daughter, name of Edy. She was birthed in 1796. She died as a babe.

In this year of 1820, I will be nineteen years of age and am very much alive. I am my mama's only surviving daughter. So then, you would think she would not want to be rid of me.

But she does. Just like lots of other folk here on Monticello. Oh, they'll not realize that too easily, I can say.

11

Master doesn't want me to go. Doesn't want my brother Beverly to go, either. I know. I can tell. Even though he's never spoken of it to me.

Not many people have spoken of it to me. Not to my face with those words—go Harriet, go. It's all sly little sayings. They sniff around me with words about it, like a fox sniffing around a henhouse.

Until this morning. What happened this morning is what made me write in this book finally. The master said write things down. It eases the heart, he said. Well, he should know. He scribbles all the time in those books of his.

I wonder what pain there is in his heart that he has to take note of so much. Something tells me there is pain there. I see it in his eyes sometimes when I'm in the same room with him and he's gazing off, thinking nobody is watching.

I'm watching him. Me. Harriet. I watch the great Thomas Jefferson all the time when he doesn't know it. And I see things others don't see. I can do that with people. Especially with white folk. They don't know how to keep what's in their hearts from showing in their eyes like we do.

Oh, something tells me these next two years, until I reach twenty-one, will be worth writing down. One thing I have promised myself, however. What I record here will be the truth as I know it to be. Not the words I have to make my mouth say to people around here because they want to hear them. And not the words I lie to myself. But the way things really be. The way that only I know they be, even though it pains me to say so.

So then, right away, here is the first truth.

I don't want to leave here when I am twenty-one. And that is as big a truth as anybody can get past their lips and still live and breathe in the Lord's good world every day.

Leave. They want me to leave like my brother Tom. Let me get it down plain in case anybody reads this book after I get done writing in it. Tom ran off. He rode off on one of the master's good horses in the middle of the night with a haversack full of salted meat and Mama's own cornbread and a fist full of gold coins. And a bottle of the master's best wine. *Vin de Ledanon*, they tell me. Nothing but the finest for brother Tom.

That was in the year 1811. I was ten years of age, and I remember Tom. Though I can't conjure up his face as well as I used to. But I recollect that he was tall and always full of the devil's own merriment. He was Mama's joy. They still speak of him down in the quarters where the servants live, on Mulberry Row.

Although what they speak of him on Mulberry Row is better said in whispers. Mammy Ursula told it to me. It goes like this.

Whenever important company came up the mountain, Tom was sent to one of the master's other plantations. Because too many visitors went away whispering about him if he stayed. Mammy says if you saw him in the shadows, that light-skinned nigra boy, standing there so tall, with his red hair tied back military fashion and his broad shoulders, why, you'd swear he was the master all over again. That's what Mammy says.

Then she laughs. "Lord knows," she says, "there be talk enough 'bout him in the papers when the master was President."

Everybody knows that. What everybody doesn't know is that there are folks walking around right on this mountain these days saying there never was a Tom. Acting like he was something Mammy conjured up over one of her concoctions. Well, I don't know if what they said in the papers was true, way back when the master was President. But there was a Tom, all right. And he was my brother. And now he's gone, and nobody's seen him in years. I suppose if I left, there are those who would say that about me, too. There never was a Harriet. It grieves me to think on it. Well, I won't. And neither will I give them the opportunity to say it.

Mammy told me how my mama carried on when Tom left. Wouldn't come out of her room for days. Her baby gone, and she didn't figure on ever seeing him again. I wonder if she'd carry on like that over me.

". . . But there be a light in her eyes anyway, when she finally did come outa that room," Mammy told me, ". . . cause she knew her baby had gone on to freedom."

Freedom. How I hate the sound of that word. It's all my mama talks about to me anymore. Oh, not directly, mind you. But in that foxy way of hers. It's like a knife in my heart every time she says the word.

And she gets the look of a demented dog in her eyes when she says it, too.

But I write here that I never knew until this morning how slippery she can be about pushing this freedom at me. It was my mistake, I calculate now, to go through the kitchen on my way out of the house. There she was, like B'rer Fox, waiting for me. The kitchen is under the south terrace.

". . . Where you off to?" she asks. Her back is to me. I make up a quick lie. Where do I go every morning this time, I ask her.

". . . To the weaver's cottage. But this is the Sabbath."

Well, of course I don't do any weaving on the Sabbath. I don't do that much weaving all week, if the truth be known. The master never chides me for not working hard. I'm going to Mammy Ursula's, I tell her.

Well, that got her turned around, all right.

"Aren't you a little old for storytelling?" she says.

I just stood there, stuffing her fresh-baked bread into my mouth. I'm learning all about B'rer Fox and B'rer Rabbit, I told her.

She squints her eyes at me then. She's too clever for her own good, my mama, if you ask me. Knows more than any nigra servant has a right to know, even though, looking at her, the last thing you'd call her was nigra. Why, she knows French and how to play the pianoforte, and she can understand all that talk of politics that goes on around here all the time. The master discusses everything with her, that's the trouble. And when he isn't, she's listening outside the dining room when he has all those important people to dine.

"Seems to me you don't need to learn anymore about B'rer Fox," she says. "You're always outfoxing me."

I knew then that I'd made a mistake coming through the kitchen, that the hot, sweet coffee and fresh bread weren't going to be worth the grief she was going to give me.

"I want you to serve Mister Randolph his breakfast," she says then.

My heart fell inside me when she said that. Like a piece of crockery on the brick floor under my feet. That's not my job, I told her. I don't have house duties.

"You do now," she says, "Your job is what I tell you it is. The master may pamper you, but I don't. And I am the mistress of Monticello."

We started in on that then. You aren't the mistress, I told her. Martha Randolph is. The master said so.

Well, that almost drove her wild.

". . . Don't you get saucy with me, miss. I've been on this place since I was two years old. This place wouldn't last a day without me. My mama ran it before me. Master couldn't do without Elizabeth Hemings when he first brought her here. And now he can't do without me. I don't care what Martha Randolph says!"

Well, she's near to crazy by now, throwing things around and waving her arms.

". . . thankful my sister Critta, or Lord be praised, my mama, dead these thirteen years now, ain't here to listen to such sass. You telling me I'm not in charge around here?"

Lordy, I was sorry I'd started all this. I didn't mean

16

that, Mama, I said. I just don't want to serve Mister Randolph. Why does he have to be served anyway? Master doesn't want servants hovering 'round him in the dining room.

". . . Master serves himself. Likes it that way. Mister Randolph is lonely."

Any man would be lonely married to Martha, I said.

She tells me to hush then, but I know she's in agreement with me on that. And I know she's forgiven me. So I followed her after she picked up a tray that was covered with a snowy white linen napkin. I walked with her through the underground corridor, past the cider room and the wine cellar. At the end of it she put the tray down on a table and started fussing over me.

"You don't go sassing Martha when she's in earshot. Could get you in trouble."

Don't care, I said. She doesn't love her husband. Doesn't live with him. Lives here. Maybe that's why he's crazier than a loon.

"Who says such things of him?"

Oh, Mama, you know everybody does, I told her.

She was taking off her white apron and tying it around me. Then she wrapped her white kerchief around my head, doing her best to stuff my blowy red hair into it. I wear my hair in one long braid down my back, but there's always wisps of hair flying all over.

". . . you know what that crazy Mister Randolph is about to do?" she asks.

She had my attention then. I do love gossip. And the servant grapevine between here and Edgehill, which is one of Mister Randolph's plantations, says

17

that Thomas Mann Randolph, son-in-law of the master, is possessed by demons. I believe in demons. They exist, I know, because Mammy Ursula told me all about them.

". . . He's about to propose to the legislature that all Virginia's slaves be freed and deported," she says.

Deported, I asked? Where to?

". . . what does it matter? Freedom is all that matters."

Oh, Lordy, I thought. She gets to talking freedom, and whatever is under that napkin will just get petrified. But I said nothing. You don't mess with words when Mama talks about freedom. You just listen.

". . . His father-in-law could have done it. He was President of these United States. What's he done for our people besides all that fancy speechifying? Sure, he asks Congress to end the slave trade. Back in 1806. And he forbade the slave trade in the new Louisiana Territory. But did he encourage them to pass that bill in Congress that would have banned slavery in all the states beyond the original thirteen? Did he?"

Now, my mama doesn't fool me. It's one thing for her to run down the master. I know she loves him. But I knew when to keep my mouth shut. If I said one word against him, she'd box my ears good.

It's just that she's got this sickness in her for thinking that if she'd had the sense of a hooty owl, she'd have stayed in France years ago when she was there with the master. Instead of coming back here. She was free in France. She'd have her precious freedom. Which to me is as incomprehensible as hair on a frog's chin.

". . . And now who does this?" she's saying.

"Thomas Mann Randolph, the person they all say is crazy. Well, if he's crazy, that man, then I'm the Queen of France. Now you go serve him. And remember, he's the Governor of Virginia. He has lots of important things on his mind. You don't sass him, or you'll hear from me."

Last thing I had on my mind was to sass him. I had all I could do to think on carrying that tray. Then, when I get up the stairway to the hall outside the dining room, who's at the end of that hall, hissing at me like a snake?

Thruston, that's who.

I set the tray down on the shelf of the revolving door the master invented so servants could leave his food without hovering around him.

"*Psst, Harriet,*" Thruston is saying. He's twenty-five and one of the pets of the household, which, if you ask me, has too many pets altogether. He's one of the master's best gardeners. He can play the fiddle like one of those French dandies Mama talks about from her days in Paris. Me and Thruston grew up together. We tumbled on these lawns with the master's grandchildren.

I have no argument with Thruston. He takes life with the ease of a hound dog. But he was the last person I wanted to run into just then. Yet there he was. Oh, Lordy, there he was, tall and sassy as ever, making hissing noises at me. I shook my head no. I waved him off. But he was more persnickety than a housefly in August. He walked right into the hall from the terrace.

19

"Since when you a house nigra?" he asks.

Since a few minutes ago, I told him. Since Mama said I was.

Well, that's enough to shut his mouth. He likes Mama. And she likes him. Lots of people around here see Thruston as no-count. Even a little daft. But that's because he talks to the flowers. Calls them "my pretty."

And the flowers grow for him. Mammy Ursula says he does good voodoo to those flowers. But we don't mention that here in the big house. Because the master, being so scientific as he is, doesn't hold with voodoo, good or otherwise.

I noticed then how Thruston was looking at me. Enough to say he's been looking at me that way too much lately. It worries me. Because I'm never going to let him sweet-talk me or put a spell on me. I'm not going to fall under any man's spell until I'm ready.

"You wanna go walkin' wif' me later?" he asked. Now, I must write it plain here. Thruston can speak as well as I or my mama can. Being that he's worked so much around and near the house, he's picked up the proper manner of speaking. But he won't use it. I'm forever making a fuss about his failure to enunciate his words proper like. And he's forever refusing to do so. Why, he's never told me.

"I might go walking with you if you stopped talking like a field darkie who didn't know any better," I said.

"I ain't changin' my way of talkin'. Not even for you, Harriet," he said.

"And why not, Thruston? Just tell me."

He ruminated a bit. "I'll tell you if'n you promise never to worry me 'bout it agin."

So I promised. And he told me.

"Why should I talk like white peoples?" he said. "Ain't never gonna get me anything. Doan wanna talk like white folk, anyway. Ain't nuthin' 'bout them I admire."

I fell silent. So that was it. Well, all right, Thruston, I said to myself. I'll never worry you about it again. I told him that I couldn't walk with him later, that I had an appointment.

"Oh, Miss High and Mighty. Wif' who?"

Never you mind, I said. Then I told him not to bring any of that garden soil in on the nice clean floors or my mama would make him sorry he ever drew breath.

"It's always my business what you do wif' your free time," he said. "You walkin' wif' somebody else?"

I felt sad then. He's been a good friend to me, always. So I smiled real pretty at him. He is light-skinned, but darker than I am. Of course, near everybody around here is darker than I am. I'm practically white. And I'm tall. And I have reddish hair. And some freckles. Which ought to give a body an idea of the trouble I'm in right off.

I wondered if Thruston ever pondered on who his daddy might be. I think not. Notions like that don't worry him like they worry me. Did I say I am bothered by it? I mark here that it stops me dead in my tracks every time the idea that Thomas Jefferson could be my daddy enters my mind.

There are days that I dare not think on it. And there are days when I can think of nothing else.

Beverly told me he was our daddy when I was twelve.

21

Said he was sure of it. Says that's why Tom ran off.

Well, I am not sure of it. I am more sure I can touch the stars in the heavens sometimes. And other times I am so afflicted by the possibility of it that I could die.

No, I told Thruston. I'm not walking out with anybody else. I just have something to do later. We can walk out this evening if you want.

That cheered him. "I'll play my fiddle for you, Harriet."

Then he pattered out. I picked up that tray and went into the dining room. And there he was at the table, Thomas Mann Randolph. Morning sun was streaming in from the skylight and dancing off the silverware. I took a deep breath and fastened my eyes on the double glass doors of the tearoom as I walked in.

I set the tray down, careful as I could. He whisked off the white napkin. ". . . Ah, Sally Hemings knows how I like my eggs." And he grabbed the dish and commenced to eat.

Eggs probably cold already, I thought. But Mama had warmed that dish good. I walked to the dumbwaiter and saw that Mama had sent up the master's best silver coffee urn. I could see my own image, it shined so. I carried it to the table and poured out the hot coffee.

He looked up at me. ". . . Harriet," he said. That's all. Just my name. I smiled, real nice like. White folks often say dim-witted things, just to start conversations with us. Some of them think we have no more brains

22

than Cromwell, our cat. And they don't know how to converse intelligently with us. Then, too, I suspect some of them feel guilty because they see we are just like they are. We smile and talk and we know how to wear different looks on our faces to suit the occasion. And they're ashamed because we're so much like them, and they've made slaves of us. So they don't know how to behave with us.

I stepped away from the table and sneaked some glances at him. No wonder he lives alone, I thought. Man has no more manners than a chicken scratching in the dirt on Mulberry Row. He slopped his biscuits in his eggs. He dipped them in his coffee. He got Mama's preserves on his fancy frock coat. One thing, though. He didn't look crazy.

There was a look in his eyes that was quite intelligent. But you can never tell with white folk.

Look at Charles Bankhead, who's married to the master's granddaughter, Anne, I reminded myself. He's crazy as a hooty owl and a drunk to boot. Rumor has it he beats poor Anne. Why, just last year the master's grandson, Thomas Jefferson Randolph, who is Anne's brother, met Bankhead in front of Leitch's store in Charlottesville on court day and accused him of beating his sister. Oh, we had trouble then. What does Bankhead do? Stabs Thomas Jefferson Randolph with a long knife.

And there's the master himself, galloping off in the middle of the night to go to the aid of his grandson. Bankhead was arrested, but he never came to trial. He left the county. Thomas Jefferson Randolph is alive and well, thank the Lord, as Martha, his mama, says, though he still bears scars. But Bankhead is always trouble, and I suspect he'll be causing more yet in this family.

He comes back here, too. I stay out of his way. I don't like the looks he gives me. He comes near me once and I'll stab him with a knife, I know that. Crazy fool that he is. Rides his horse right into the barroom in Charlottesville to get his liquor. And he looks sane as a preacher. You never can tell with white folk.

". . . Harriet," Randolph said. "I'm speaking to you."

Yessir.

". . . Talk to me," he said. "Don't give me that stupid darkie routine. I know you Hemings, especially Sally's children. You are anything but stupid."

Talk to him! I stood there and fidgeted with Mama's apron like I didn't have the brains of a possum. No white folk ever asked you to converse with them while they were eating. Ignored you like a piece of furniture, that's what they did. Why he couldn't do that, I don't know. I'd just as soon be regarded as a chair as talk to him. Mama would skin me alive. What had I done wrong? What should I do now?

". . . Stay, stay," he said. And he's waving his fork around like a saber. So I stayed. The fact that the man is the Governor of Virginia doesn't put me off as much as the fact that he is white and wanted to talk to me. While he was eating.

So then he started talking. Told me how tired he was. And how he got in so late last night, wet as a drowned porcupine. There had been a bad storm, and he'd forged the swollen river and came in soaked to

24

the skin. "Well, your mama took care of me. Sent down to the kitchen for a late supper. Then I stayed up 'til all hours talking with your master about his grand and all-consuming passion. You know what that is?"

I said yessir. I know. What, he asks. I said the university he's building. He says it's a constant gratification to his sight.

Well, that got him almost choking on his coffee. "Where'd you learn such a word?" he asked.

My tutor, I said. Mr. Oglesby, who teaches your older boys in Charlottesville, comes here once a week to tutor me. And Beverly.

He ruminated a bit then. "You're as white as any of them around here," he said.

Why he had to bring that up, I don't know. Nothing but trouble comes from that kind of talk. And then it came to me that he might want my favors. No. It couldn't be. No man, white or nigra, ever dares to take liberties with me around here. I am Harriet Hemings. I am protected always. There is a mantle of protection around me because of who I am. Everybody knows that. Lots of the young nigra men on Mulberry Row are jealous of me because of it. Especially Isabel's Davie. He calls me uppity.

He just went on sipping his coffee, real calm like. "You look just like him. Anybody ever tell you?"

Oh, Lordy, Lordy, what was happening now? Man wanted trouble, that's what he wanted.

"Does he think people are so stupid they don't see it?" Oh, he's chattering away, just like a magpie, mumbling it almost to himself. But I can hear it all right.

25

"My sainted father-in-law," he said. "Admired in the whole country. And the world. And here at Monticello he's laid a trap for himself. You know about traps, Harriet Hemings?"

My brother Beverly traps muskrats, I told him.

"Ha!" And he laughed. "I'm talking about the traps we humans set for ourselves. Spend our whole lives making them. What pains we take. Sometimes those traps are made of material from the briar patch. And sometimes . . ." He looked at me with a peculiar gleam in his eyes.

"Sometimes they are made of velvet."

Mad, I thought. I don't care if he is the Governor of Virginia.

"I could never come up to him. Years ago he had a machine made to measure his strength. No one was stronger than I in those days. But he . . . he was stronger. And he was sixty-seven then. And already retired from the presidency."

Yessir, I said.

"Are you making a trap for yourself here at Monticello, Harriet Hemings?"

I didn't answer.

"Your mama tells me you don't want to take your freedom when your time comes."

So there it was. The real reason Mama sent me to serve him. So he could talk up freedom to me. Oh, I was madder than a wet porcupine!

"You like being a slave?" he asked.

Slave? Me? I said nothing. He was watching me, so I kept my face from showing anything. I couldn't stop my eyes, though. They said things. I couldn't help it. And he saw, too.

"What's wrong?" he asked.

"I'm not a slave," I said.

He laughed then. He threw his head back. "What are you, then?"

"I'm Harriet Hemings." My eyes were getting tears in them.

"Yes, you're Harriet Hemings." But he didn't say it unkindly. He is most kind, most attentive. "Sally Hemings' little girl. Tutored. Dressed most properly. Does a little work in the weaver's cottage every morning. Lives upstairs on the third floor. Like a household pet."

I said nothing. What could I say?

"You know how to speak well, how to read and write. How to behave in a most amiable and agreeable fashion. Can you curtsy?"

I said I could.

"Curtsy for me."

I dropped a perfect curtsy. He nodded solemnly. Watching me all the while with those innocent blue eyes. "You're still a slave, Harriet Hemings," he said softly.

I could not keep the tears from my eyes.

He wants to know, then, why I am giving my mama trouble about leaving when my time comes. I told him I did not want to leave. He nodded and looked into his coffee cup like there was gold at the bottom.

"Don't be a fool," he said. He just about growled it. His voice came from someplace deep inside him.

27

Like thunder coming over the Blue Ridge. "We all like it here. But this place is a trap. It's him, isn't it. Your master."

"I love Master Jefferson," I said.

"Why?"

"He's kind to me."

"Kind, eh? Well, kindness is not freedom. And security is not freedom. Freedom is often lonely. Nobody takes care of you. You take care of yourself. You think for yourself. You do dim-witted things, and you are sorry for them. You pay for them. But there is no feeling in the world like freedom."

Again I said nothing.

"The way you people around here feel about this place is wrong," he said. "Slavery is wrong. I am going to introduce a resolution in the legislature that all Virginia's slaves are to be freed and deported. You understand?"

I said yessir, my mama explained that to me.

He nodded. "She understands the meaning of freedom, your mama. Even though he's got her hog-tied here."

People sure do go on about this freedom thing, I was thinking. And then he asked me what I thought about his resolution.

Lordy. No white person, except Thomas Jefferson, ever asked me what I thought about anything. The master once asked me what I thought about his storytelling.

Once, when I was a child, I hid behind a cupboard to hear the stories he was telling his grandchildren. He found me there, sent the children to bed, and took me on his knee and asked what I thought of his stories. And then he told one just for me. It was about sailing ships.

I think your resolution is a fine thing, sir, I said.

He scowled. "You want your children to be slaves?"

Slaves? My children? They wouldn't be slaves, I told him. They'd be treated like me.

To mark the truth here, however, I never thought about my children.

"They'd be slaves," he said again. "Worse than you. By then your master will be dead. And who's to care about whether your children are slaves or not. Or if they're sold or not."

Well, the man had me there, just like a fox caught in a leg trap.

"But you're going to free Virginia's slaves," I said.

He got up then. Threw down his napkin. "My legislation won't get passed," he said. "I will try, but it won't. The pro-slavery people in this state are too strong. Look at my father-in-law. He can't make his mind up about slavery. Hates it, yes. Says it's a wolf America has by the ears. And that we can no longer hold onto it. But neither can we let it go. What does that tell you, Harriet Hemings? You'll be a slave here forever if you don't take your chance when your time comes."

He moved away from the table. I could see his image in the shiny surface of the coffee urn. Getting smaller. I don't like hearing anybody detract from the master's character, but I knew I couldn't argue with a white man.

"There's a world out there, Harriet Hemings," he

said. "I promised your mama I'd speak to you like this. She always treats me with respect. Here in this house, not many people do. Here in this house, I feel like the proverbial silly bird who cannot feel at ease among the swans. My wife prefers to live here, with her adored father, rather than live with me. I am in the shadow of my father-in-law. His shadow falls over everyone here. Why do you think I don't stay here? I can't. But when I am here, your mama gives my shadow its own territory. You heed my words, girl. You have a right to the freedom Thomas Jefferson says all people are entitled to. Now you may go."

I curtsied again for him. It was the very least I could do. He nodded, then he left the room. And there was only one person shining out of the silver coffee urn. Me.

Alone in that room I was terrified. I looked around. I love that dining room. It has quiet blue walls and sparkling white woodwork. It's a genteel and agreeable room, and it has a story about it, a story my mama told me.

I thought on the story while I got the dishes onto the tray.

One day in 1781, the British came riding up the mountain. They came looking for the master. It was June. He was dining alone. "I was a little girl," my mama told me. "A militia captain, Jack Jouett, rode all night to warn the master after he saw those green-coated devils at the Cuckoo Tavern.

"The British were led by Lieutenant Colonel Banastre Tarleton. A dandy. A bad man. His badness was known throughout the colonies. My master sent his family away to safety, then sat down to breakfast. He watched the British coming through his telescope.

"When they got closer, he gathered some things and rode off on a horse over the mountain. My half brother, Martin, opened the front door. One of the British soldiers put a gun to Martin's head. Where was Thomas Jefferson, they wanted to know. The man who wrote the Declaration of Independence. We want to hang him. But Martin wouldn't tell. I cried. I was so frightened. I thought they would kill my brother in front of my eyes."

That is my mother's story. And I write it down here. She told me that story and many others at bedtime. I grew up with such stories. They are part of my life.

What if the British had hung him, I thought, as I piled the last of the dishes on the tray. Would I be here this morning? Is he my father?

My mama would never tell me. She does not speak of such things. Slave women never speak of their children's fathers to them. And slave children always take the condition of slavery. They take their mother's lot.

I set the silver coffee urn back on the dumbwaiter. How can I leave this place, I thought, looking around the dining room. I love it here. Beverly hasn't left yet, and he's twenty-two. He's waiting for the right moment, he says.

When is the right moment? When Mr. Oglesby has no more to teach us? When I get tired of the beautiful gardens, the fields and orchards? The deep forests of the Blue Ridge?

When I am no longer entranced by the French pier

mirror in the parlor? When the seven-day clock in the entranceway no longer charms me?

When I get weary of studying the collection of Indian curios brought back by Lewis and Clark?

How can I leave all this? More to the point, how can I leave the man whose shadow falls over it all? The man with the burning blue eyes and the thick white hair, the tall, kind man who rides his horse like a god and who puts his arm around me and tells me stories of Mama when she was a child.

The man who gave me this journal, who plays the violin while his younger grandchildren dance around him. The man who gives brilliant speeches and who has sudden silences, which I sense are filled with pain. Especially when he looks at my mother.

I mark down here in my book, where I have vowed to tell the truth, that in that very genteel dining room, I prayed. Please, God, don't let Mister Randolph be right. Please, God, let him be crazy. Everybody says he is crazy. His wife won't live with him. Doesn't that make him crazy, God?

But I knew, inside me, where you know things, that Thomas Mann Randolph was not crazy. And I knew I would have to think on what he said. Oh, but please, God, don't let him be right.

April 1820

Oh, Lordy, I thought that what happened to me yesterday in that very genteel dining room was bad. But what happened after I left is worse.

But first I must record here some of the madness that goes on in this house. We have no right, any of us, to call anybody crazy.

It goes like this: My grandma, born in 1735 and dead these thirteen years, was the mistress of John Wayles. Mama says he was most agreeable, full of pleasantry and good humor. Well, he sure must have been, because he buried three wives. He had four living children. The master's wife, Martha, was one of them.

But that didn't seem to be enough for Mister Wayles. Oh, no. Seems he still had a lot of pleasantries left in him. After he buried his third wife, he took Elizabeth Hemings, his mulatto slave and my grandma, as his woman.

He must have been agreeable to Grandma Elizabeth Hemings. Because she bore him six children. And she already had six from a slave man.

Didn't bother Grandma Elizabeth any, though. She just went about the business of birthing like it was no more trouble than falling off a log. While white women all around her were dying from it. The master's own wife died from the effects of it, my mama says. But not my grandma.

Well, just short of two years after John Wayles' daughter Martha married my master, Mister Wayles died in 1773. And Martha and the master inherited 135 slaves from him.

My grandma was one of them. So were ten of her twelve children.

And that's how the Hemings got to Monticello. Most slaves don't have last names. They take the name of their master. Grandma Elizabeth was the first female of the family to have an English name. My grandma's children took her name. Hemings.

It was my grandma's daddy's name. And he was the captain of an English sailing vessel that put in at the town of Williamsburg at the time when Grandma Elizabeth was about to be born. Her mother, my great-grandmother, was full-blooded African.

So, then. Captain Hemings was my great-grandfather on my mama's side. John Wayles was my grandfather. Both white men. But there is more.

Because my Grandma Elizabeth bore six children by John Wayles, my mama, who is one of them, was half sister to Martha Wayles Skelton. Who is dead now. And who was Thomas Jefferson's wife.

Hemings have been on Monticello ever since Mister Wayles died. Of the six children by John Wayles that Grandma Elizabeth brought here, the "light Hemings" were Mama's brother Peter and sister Critta, who died. The master freed Mama's older brothers Robert and James. Although James went and killed himself a while back. Which shows what this freedom can do to you. And Thenia, Mama's other sister, the master sent to James Monroe, who is his neighbor.

I mark all this down here to keep it straight. Sometimes I get it powerful mixed up in my head. There're so many Hemings around here, nobody knows who they are half the time. Except the master. He keeps track of everything. He knows. I can see in his eyes that he knows just who we all are. Although there's times I'd swear, just looking at him, that he's wondering how it all happened. And figuring just what he's gonna do about it.

But I have to get back to what happened yesterday morning. And so, here comes another truth.

My brother Beverly isn't leaving this place for one reason. He wants the master to send him to the university the master is building.

Beverly is one smart boy. But I am smarter. Because I have suspected this about him all along. No, he hasn't let one word about it pass his lips to me. But he's always trying to show the master how clever he is. And that's what he was doing yesterday morning.

He outdid himself yesterday morning to prove how smart he was. He launched a balloon. And that's where I was headed when Mama caught me in the kitchen. To help him.

35

After I got done serving Mister Randolph, I escaped the house finally. Outside, I stood on the southern breezeway, looking at the plantation, which was all laid out before me.

Down the slope of lawns was Mulberry Row. I could see the woodsmoke rising out of the cabin chimneys. And, as I stood there, breathing it all in, I felt that it was mine. The whole place. Everything. The dewy flower beds, the great orchards, the acres of tobacco and cotton and wheat and the pastures full of horses and cattle.

All five thousand acres of it. Mine. And I knew how Thomas Jefferson must feel, seeing it.

From where I stood, I could see the workshops on Mulberry Row, the washhouse, the bakery, the tanning shop, the storage houses, the nailery and carpenter's shop to name just a few.

And I stood thinking how Thomas Jefferson could not live without his nigra servants, from Burwell, his valet, and Joe Fossett, the blacksmith, to the ones who work in the fields. And John Hemings, who is my mama's half brother and such an expert cabinetmaker. And dozens and dozens of others. Even I, who tell him things for his Farm Book.

So he told Mister Randolph, the master, that slavery is a wolf America holds by the ears, did he? Well, no wonder he thinks America can't let it go. Oh, why do I think such things about him? I love him, I know I do. And to show how much, I write down here and now another truth.

The nigra servants on this place are well treated. And well clothed and fed. Mama says the master, like his father, Peter Jefferson, has never used a whip on one of his servants. And no one goes cold or hungry. Or works for a year to earn one ragged garment. Or shivers under vermin-infested blankets in winter.

And Mr. Oglesby, my tutor, says that the master runs his plantation with the same exactness he runs his political life. There is order to life here. And now I must tell about Beverly's balloon.

I heard voices on the morning air. And then my eyes found them in the distance. Two figures. And I thought my heart would burst inside me. I ran down the slopes, my long braid bouncing on my back. My skirts flapped. There, ahead of me in the distance, at the end of Mulberry Row, they walked up the green hill, the two men. And, oh, my heart leapt inside me to see the tall, lean man with his horse, Eagle, the man with his hair tied back, wearing heavy boots and a tricorn hat.

Next to him was Beverly, holding a patchwork quilt of silk in his arms. He had made his balloon in secret, begging bits and pieces of silk from Mama. I had sat with him many an evening in the carpenter's shop, where he worked, while he constructed the basket to hold the brazier in which he would burn straw to make hot air for his balloon.

They did not know I followed. I stopped at the washhouse, out of breath. Oh, why hadn't I come sooner? If I had, the balloon would be launched already. Now the master caught him in the act.

He wanted it to be a surprise. We both know the love the master has for the scientific. Why, it was from his library that Beverly got all the information for his balloon. From the master's books on Galileo. And from copies of the letters he'd sent home from France in 1783, when the first balloon flights began.

How Beverly had studied those letters and pamphlets on ballooning! There is a madness for ballooning now in America. Beverly read me accounts in the local papers of the balloon club at the College of William and Mary. And he told me how, in 1783, a sheep, a duck, and a rooster were sent aloft in a balloon in Versailles. And how men have flown since, in Europe and America.

I peeked around the washhouse. I did not want to intrude. Another truth I write here now. I am very shy around the master. I know he loves me. His face is not stern when he looks at me. His fine features seem to soften when I come into his sight. And, oh, I do crave his attention. But I never force myself into his presence until he smiles at me and gestures that I should come forward. I prefer to watch him from a distance.

They stopped on the hill, green with newly sprouting growth. The master dropped Eagle's reins, and they stood talking. I saw the master put his arm out to touch Beverly's shoulder and, oh, I felt so jealous.

Beverly was holding his silk balloon close to his chest and he backed away. And it was then that I heard the conversation I wish my ears had never heard at all.

Beverly, you know I can't, says the master. And Beverly asks him why he can't. Because, the master says, I just can't. Don't ask me why. Haven't I given you everything? The best of tutors? Haven't I allowed you to use my library? Haven't I given you freedom on this place?

But you don't understand, Beverly says then. I'm not a child anymore. All that was all right for when I was a child. But there's nothing more Mr. Oglesby can teach me, and I want to go further with my studies.

Ah, there it was. What I'd figured all along. Said out. It broke my heart, I can tell you.

"I have a good mind," Beverly is saying.

"I know," the master answers. "I see how beautifully you've made your balloon."

My brother is angry now. "You haven't seen anything yet," he shouts. "I wanted to fly it before you found out. Like the students at William and Mary. I wanted to surprise you. To make you proud of me!"

And then Beverly turns away, and the master puts a hand on his arm. "I am proud of you, Beverly. I'm sorry I ruined your surprise. Let me see the basket. What will you put in the brazier to produce hot air? Hickory sticks or straw?"

Now Beverly is still turned away from him. "None of that," he says.

"What, then?"

And then Beverly tells him. "Wine."

And the great Thomas Jefferson cannot believe what he is hearing. "Wine?" he asks. "Wine?"

"Yes." And Beverly faces him now. "I will dip a sponge in wine and set it on fire. It will produce a better heat than wood or straw. It will make my balloon rise to a great height."

"Wine?" the master says again. "And how did you come to think of wine?"

"It burns," Beverly says. "I have been experimenting with it."

"That could be dangerous," the master says.

"I'm careful."

"Wine!" Thomas Jefferson, the great man himself, shakes his head. And, oh, I am so proud of Beverly I could burst! Then the master asks him where he got the wine. "Have you been at my Montepulcian? My Perpignan? My Riversalte?"

And Beverly shakes his head. "Just your French claret."

"Just my French claret?" And the master is amazed. He shakes his head. He laughs. "Very well, you deserve a chance to set off your balloon. Even though I ought to box your ears for taking my good wine. I'll leave you be. I'll go for my ride. And when I come back, everyone will come running to tell me about it. If I don't see it floating up there over the mountains."

Then Beverly says no, he doesn't want to fly it anymore. Why, the master asks. And Beverly turns on him, angry.

"Why do you think? What good will it do? You don't think I'm smart enough to go to the university. Nothing I do will convince you!"

"Beverly," the master says softly, "I know you are smart enough to go to the university."

"Then let me go," Beverly says. He doesn't say it as much as he begs it. And it makes my heart sore to think how Beverly is begging, proud as he always is.

"I told you I can't," the master says again.

"You can!" Oh, that brother of mine is as stubborn

as a house fly in August. "It's your university," he says. "You built it! You were President of the United States! You can do anything!"

And, oh, we have trouble now, I'm thinking, standing there. I was frightened because Beverly was showing so much anger. But the master was calm.

"Did I ever tell you the story of my old mentor and law teacher, George Wythe?" he says.

"You go to hell!" Beverly shouts at him. "I don't want any more of your stories! I'm not a child to be lulled with stories!"

Well, I thought the sky would fall on us all then. I could scarcely believe my ears. I held my breath, waiting for God's fist to come down on my brother's head. I was certain that no one in his life had ever told the great Thomas Jefferson to go to hell. And Mama would switch Beverly good if she knew.

I saw the master take a step back. And the two of them stood there against that green hill and blue sky like two dogs circling on Mulberry Row. Mammy Ursula would say that what was between them now was bad voodoo. Bad spirits.

"Put that thing down," the master says. And his voice is cold as the earth on a January morning. And as hard. Beverly obeys. He sets the balloon down.

"Now come here," the master says.

Well, Beverly does, all right, I have to give him that. He goes and stands straight in front of the master. Then Thomas Jefferson reaches out and grabs his shoulder and shakes him real gentle like. "I'm glad no one heard you, Beverly," he says, "or I'd have to punish

41

you. Now this is a true story, and I want you to listen."

Beverly is just looking at the ground.

"I said will you listen. Or is your mind closed? A man with a good mind always listens."

"I have a good mind," Beverly says.

"Then prove it to me. Or are you afraid of what I have to say?"

"I'm not afraid of anything." And Beverly looks him straight in the eye.

"Good." Thomas Jefferson drops his hands to his sides and commences to tell his story, which, near as I can recall, goes like this:

"In 1806 I was still President. I received a letter from a friend in Richmond telling me that my old law teacher, George Wythe, was dying. And that arsenic had been found in the bedroom of his grandnephew, George Sweney. Wythe was a widower, and he had a mulatto housekeeper named Lydia Broadnax."

Well, at the mention of a mulatto housekeeper, Beverly's ears perk up, all right. And the master goes on.

"Lydia had a son named Michael Brown, and it was common knowledge that the boy was Wythe's illegitimate son by her. Wythe loved the boy and treated him well."

What story was this, I wondered. I had never heard it before. Then the master's voice went hoarse. "Just as I love you, Beverly," he says. "As I loved your brother Tom. Only Wythe went a step further. He took his boy about with him. He taught him Latin and Greek, mathematics and astronomy. He wanted to prove that this child was not only capable of learning but the possessor of a brilliant mind. He had no children by his previous marriages."

"What's this got to do with me?" Beverly asks.

"It has *much* to do with you! And I will not be interrupted again!"

Well, I shivered then. I just felt goose bumps all over. Never had I heard such a tone in the master's voice in my whole life. And if he ever used it on me, I know I would shrivel up and die right there in front of him.

Beverly didn't shrivel up, but he did nod. And the master continued.

"Wythe took his grandnephew under his wing. Like a son. But he had a will written on April 20, 1803, in which he left Lydia Broadnax his house and a good portion of his property. He left Michael half his bank stock and instructed that I . . . the President of the United States, be in charge of the maintenance, education, and other benefit of his young mulatto son."

Thomas Jefferson stops talking now so that it should sink in to Beverly's mind. "The other bank stock he left to Sweney," he said. "The will said that Sweney should get it all if Michael Brown died first. Well, Sweney poisoned them all, Lydia and Michael and George Wythe. He was charged with murder and sent to jail."

I moved a little closer to the end of the washhouse to hear better. The master's voice was getting low.

"The trial was like a carnival in Richmond. It was unheard of that a man should leave his house to his mulatto housekeeper and half his bank stock to her son and request that the President of the United States

43

be responsible for that son's education. George Wythe went against all the unwritten rules of society. Do you understand?"

"No, sir." Oh, that Beverly was sullen.

"Then I will tell you," the master says. "Lydia Broadnax did not die. But because, under Virginia law, no nigra can testify against a white, Sweney was acquitted. Leading men in Richmond rushed to defend him. The indictment against him was quashed without a trial. And a murderer was allowed to go free because my dear friend and mentor, a signer of the Declaration of Independence, did not try to hide the fact that he had a mulatto mistress and could not disown his son. Now do you understand?"

Beverly just nodded.

Thomas Jefferson backed away. "This is the way of things, Beverly," and he is very sad when he says it. "I cannot change them. When I wrote my declaration, I tried. But there were those who would have seceded from the yet unformed union if my phrases about doing away with slavery were not struck from the document. You think I do not know what is right and wrong? Answer me!"

"No, sir," Beverly says real quiet like.

"I know right and wrong. And I dream dreams. Just like you. But every time I dream those dreams I remember my old friend George Wythe. And I am brought back to the way things are. Beverly, listen well when I tell you this. I tremble for my country when I reflect that God is just. But I am one man. I cannot change the way of things."

Beverly did not answer.

"They will change," Thomas Jefferson says. "Perhaps not in my lifetime. But they will change. Either by the generous energy of our own minds or by some bloody process I tremble to think about. Do you hear me, Beverly?"

"Yes, sir."

Thomas Jefferson nods now and looks at Eagle's reins, which are on the ground. "Get my reins, please," he says. And Beverly scoops them up and hands them to him. And I saw their hands touch. And I could feel the hours passing across the face of eternity it seemed, before my brother starts to cry. His shoulders shake and he leans toward the master. And the master takes him by the shoulders and embraces him.

"Are you going to fly away from me, Beverly?" he asks. "Is that what you're going to do in that thing?"

Beverly shakes his head no.

"You don't have to fly away, you know," the master tells him. "You're free to go whenever you want. I was hoping you'd stay, however. You know that, don't you?"

Beverly nodded yes. I saw the master touch his face. Then he released Beverly. And my brother moves instantly, to hold the horse while the master mounted. Then he stands there looking up at the regal figure of the man who is smiling down at him.

"Fly your balloon, Beverly," the master says. "Light your sponge of wine. And when I come back, I want to hear all about it."

Then, as if that isn't enough to make a body melt into the earth right there, he reaches down from Eagle and ruffles Beverly's hair. "Wine, eh?" he says. And he clips Beverly on the side of the face, playful like. "Fly the damn thing," he says.

Never in my life have I ever heard the master swear. Mama says she never did, either. Then he wheels around on Eagle and gallops across the green meadow and into the woods.

Well, by then, tears were coming down my face. I mark that truth here. How could you not love a master like that, I asked myself. As if I needed asking. I leaned against the corner of the washhouse and watched him ride off. Then I brought my eyes back to Beverly. He was on the ground, kneeling over his balloon. What would he do now? Was he snared, once again, in the velvet trap of the master's love? Like he snared musk-rats? But I brushed my tears away and ran toward him.

"Beverly!"

He looks up as I get near, but he continues working. "I'm sorry I'm late. Mama made me serve Mister Randolph breakfast."

He was taking something out of the basket of the balloon, something wrapped in burlap. He unwrapped it, and there was a bottle of wine.

Well, of course, I pretended I didn't know anything about this wine. "What do you have there?" I ask.

"What does it look like?" Oh, he was in an ornery mood, all right.

"Looks like wine," I said. "French wine. You going to drink it?"

He sneered. "Do you think I'd go through all the trouble of stealing it to drink it? If I wanted to drink I can get all the rum I want."

"You don't drink rum, Beverly. You've never even had whiskey."

"Haven't I? You saw me last Christmas when our father gave it out."

"No, I didn't. And you'd better never let Mama see you drinking, either. What's the wine for?"

"To burn."

I acted real surprised. "The master's good claret?"

"Stop calling him master. He's your father. Call him that."

I was surprised now. Didn't have to pretend. "Do you call him father?"

"I do if I want. He lets me say almost anything to him."

"Did he admit he's our father?"

"He doesn't have to. He said he loved me. That's enough."

I nodded. He was right about that, leastways. I watched him open the wine. The balloon, which was about three feet around, was fluttering on the ground. Beverly popped the cork of the claret and held the bottle under his nose and sniffed. "Ah, I'm sure this will do."

"Do for what?"

"Hand me that sponge there, will you, sister, and stop asking stupid questions."

The sponge was large. He poured wine on it. "Did you tell anybody about this balloon?"

"I can keep a secret. I'm not a silly girl with a loose tongue."

"Did Mama ask where you were off to?"

"I lied to her."

47

"Hand me my flints now."

He set the soaked sponge in the basket and rubbed the flints together to get sparks. "Get back now, Harriet!"

I moved back. The sponge took fire and I muffled a scream. The flames grew stronger, forcing hot air into the patchwork of silk. In no time at all it was billowing into shape.

"Look at that!" Beverly danced with glee. The small basket danced, too, on the ground. "I knew it would work!" He grabbed the basket as it lifted into the air. He held onto it, guiding it upward until he was standing on tiptoe. Then he let it go.

"Look at that! Look, Harriet!" And he put his arm around my shoulder, and we watched as the balloon, with the fire from the wine-soaked sponge, rose higher and higher into the blue April morning.

Beverly could scarcely hold himself down, either. He danced and whooped and carried on like he'd taken leave of his senses. He ran across the green meadow. And I ran behind him. "I did it! I told him I could do it!"

Well, by now people were coming out of the cabins all up and down Mulberry Row, pointing and laughing at Beverly's balloon. Women were laughing and holding each other. Men came running toward Beverly, clapping him on the shoulder.

"Jesus be praised!" one woman said.

"The French claret be praised!" Beverly yelled. Well, that was downright blasphemous. And on the Sabbath, too. But nobody much noticed. They were all standing around gazing up at the heavens as that

48

balloon drifted away, headed over toward the Blue Ridge Mountains. They stood there and watched it until they could see it no more. Until it was just a speck in the sky. Then they turned and made their way back to their cabins. They were all talking about Beverly's balloon and how that Beverly was one smart boy and how they would tell the master when he returned.

"What do you think our father will do when he finds out?" I asked my brother.

"He already knows." Beverly skipped. "He found me with it before you came before."

"Oh, Beverly! You wanted to make it a surprise!"

"Doesn't matter. He asked me all about it. He was proud of me, he said. He said that if I got the balloon in the air, that would prove how smart I was and he would let me go to the university."

Well, I felt as if I were hit in the face with a bucket of cold water then. I stopped dead in that field and stared at my brother like he'd gone daft. A big hand had a grip right around my heart.

"He said he'd let you go to the university?" I repeated.

"That's right. That's what old Thomas Jefferson said. How do you like that, Harriet?"

Well, I didn't like it. I didn't like it at all. Because I knew he was lying. I heard what the master had said to him earlier, and it wasn't that he could go to the university. So why was he doing this, then? Was it possible he believed that once the master heard about the balloon, he'd change his mind and let Beverly go?

That would be terrible, I thought. Hope is cruel.

And for Beverly, it is the cruelest thing ever. Because as long as he had hope he'd never take his freedom and go. And after what I'd heard from the master this morning, that story about Mr. Wythe and his mulatto mistress, I knew Beverly had to go.

The master was telling him he could do no more for him. Didn't Beverly have brains enough to know that? How could he be so smart, to get a balloon in the air, and not figure that out?

He had to take his freedom and go. That was the only hope for him. Oh, Lordy, Lordy, I thought standing there. I'm starting to think like Mama now.

But I knew Beverly had to go. Because every day he stayed, that hope inside him would turn like a stone in his chest. Until it squashed down everything else inside him. And it would show in his eyes. The color of those slate flints of his.

And then I had another thought, standing there. What if he was only saying this because he couldn't bear to let me know the truth? That was even worse. Because we'd shared everything up until now. All our childhood joys and sorrows. That would mean Beverly had already shut me out of his life. And then he'd start to shut everybody else out, too.

And I know, from life on this plantation, that sadness shared is a burden lessened. Oh, I don't have any burdens. Leastways I didn't up until now. But I know all those nigra servants on Mulberry Row. And I know that if they hadn't been able to share their sadnesses over the years, they would all have given up and blown away by now. Like Beverly's balloon.

So what was Beverly doing now? I ran across the

field to catch up with him. He was doing cartwheels and yelping out his gladness over his balloon. And his yelps of joy cut like a knife in my heart.

People can't live lies. Oh, they can for a few days, a few weeks. Maybe a few months, even. But soon the lies take over and squeeze all the life out of you so you can't breathe anymore. So you can't sleep. So you can't even talk to people because you don't know what words are truth anymore and what words are lies.

"You see that balloon everybody?" Beverly is yelling. "You see it? It was the claret! The French wine! Old Thomas Jefferson like to die when I told him about the wine. Now he knows how smart I am!"

I was glad he was running ahead of me. At least he couldn't see the tears coming down my face.

April 1820
That same day

What can I say about Beverly? I felt so distressed seeing him take on like he had no more sense than a cricket that I left him and walked back through Mulberry Row. I didn't know where I was heading, but I ended up at Mammy Ursula's cabin.

It's a wood cabin, and on the porch she keeps the baskets she weaves. She's an old woman now. Been on this place for as long as my mama can remember. She has no more chores except to tell stories to the little ones and help birth a baby every so often. To keep her hands busy, she weaves her baskets.

Everybody on the place uses Mammy's baskets. What the white folk don't know is that into each of her baskets she weaves a pattern to keep away witches.

Mammy keeps the nigra folktales and practices alive around here. And she dispenses advice. On how to cast and be rid of spells. She also distributes her potions. From her I learned that a witch can transform herself into any animal she chooses, beast or bird.

I learned how a witch can creep through a keyhole. And how, if a rabbit crosses your path, it changes your luck. And that if you set out on a journey and a hooty owl screeches on your left side, you must return and set out again or expect bad things to happen. Mammy told me all about dreams, too, and what they mean. Why, if it weren't for her, I'd never know that when you first hear the whippoorwill in the spring, you should turn head over heels three times to prevent backache all year long.

My own mama says all this is stuff and nonsense. That's because the master doesn't hold with nigra folklore. He's too educated. And my mama thinks she is, too. But I notice she isn't above using Mammy's remedies to get rid of pleurisy and rheumatism. Why, there is a whole catalogue of human infirmities that Mammy can cure. And Mama learned them from her.

I knew Mammy wouldn't be at church this Sabbath morning. She won't go down the mountain to church because she says the Baptist minister cheats her out of the true Christian message. And she won't be segregated the way nigras have to be in white people's churches.

Besides, the minister there only tells all black folk to obey their masters. No, Mammy will go to the afternoon song and preaching meeting the servants on this place hold late on the Sabbath afternoon.

I've been, and I can't say they aren't edifying. There's always a nigra preacher, making his rounds of neighboring plantations with special passes to preach.

53

Nigra preachers are the best. And held in high esteem. They tell stories about Old Testament heroes and get positively spooky with their tales of hell. No white preacher can hold a crowd like they can.

I hear some white people's churches in Virginia even have nigra preachers in regular because they prefer them to their own kind.

Well, anyway, I got onto the porch of Mammy's house and stood and listened. She was storytelling, and I didn't want to interrupt.

". . . But the Wolf, he call his son and say, 'Let us throw B'rer Rabbit in the river.' B'rer Rabbit say, 'Thas right. Throw me in there because I ain't washed my skin in a long time.' The Wolf say, 'No, let's throw him in the fire.'

". . . 'Throw me in the fire. Then I would jump right over it,' say B'rer Rabbit. The Wolf, he say, 'No, let's throw him in the briar patch!' Well, B'rer Rabbit say, 'Don't, Wolf. Don't throw me in the briar patch!' And B'rer Wolf, he take that B'rer Rabbit and throw him in the briar patch! B'rer Rabbit say, 'Ping, ping. This is the place my mama and daddy borned me. And this is where I'se gonna stay!' "

I peeked in the door. Oh, I'd heard such stories so many times from Mammy Ursula. And somehow, by the tone in her voice, she makes them new each time. 'Course, I know now that I am beyond the days when such stories about a wily rabbit outwitting a stupid wolf can make me happy. But I also know that such stories are carefully handed down in the slave community. They are used to teach slave children that they can survive, too, just like B'rer Rabbit.

They can survive all kinds of humiliations. And tragedies. The nigra mamas all send their children to Mammy Ursula on Sabbath morning to hear these stories. They are as important to their upbringing as church-going.

"Go, now," I heard Mammy shooing the children off. "I gots to polish my pot."

Then, like a river, they came rushing by me, six or eight of them, screeching. And I heard Mammy say, ". . . You kin come in now, Harriet Hemings."

There she was in her rocking chair. I kissed her old, round face. She was wearing her blue checkered homespun dress and a new white apron for the Sabbath. Her turban was bright red. And wisps of gray hair pushed out from it.

"How nice you come to see me. Come sit next to me so I kin see how you're doin'."

I sat. "You're not doin' so good, I kin see. What's the matter?"

"Everything, Mammy," I told her.

She laughed then. "Chile, you doan know what trouble is, thas your trouble."

She started a little chant. "Her face look lak a coffeepot, her nose look lak de spout. Her mouf look lak a fiah-place, wid de ashes takin out."

It was an old rhyme she used to make children smile.

"That old Martha Randolph givin' you a bad time agin?"

"No, Mammy."

"How's your mama?"

"Tolerable."

She nodded, waiting. "Go ahead. I'se listinin'."

55

"It's Beverly."

She sighed. "I heard 'bout the balloon. One of the chillens comes runnin' in here shoutin' all 'bout how Beverly set off a balloon. And we stood on the porch an' watched. You afraid you brother's gonna fly right off in that balloon, Harriet?"

"No, Mammy, I'm afraid he's never going to leave this place."

She said nothing for a minute.

"He told me . . ." Oh, Lordy, I couldn't make myself say the words. "He told me that the master promised him he could go to the university if he got that balloon up."

Her eyes, so usually bright, were dark with wisdom. "Thomas Jefferson say that? He's gonna let one of Sally Hemings' boys go to the university?"

"No, Mammy, he never said it. I heard him tell Beverly myself this morning that Beverly couldn't go. He can't send him. I was listening. Behind the washhouse. Only Beverly doesn't know I heard."

She closed her eyes for an awfully long minute then. "That boy shudda been off this place a long time ago," she says.

"He won't go, Mammy. He isn't ever going to go."

"He'll go."

I looked at her. Her eyes were still closed, like she was incantating a spell.

"How do you know? All he does is loll around the master's library and read and talk about the stupid university. How do you know?"

"He'll go," she said again, like she knew something I didn't. I think she was plotting, sitting there like

56

that. "You send him to me," she said. "Tell him I wants to see him. He ain't been 'round to see me since Christmas."

"Oh, thank you, Mammy!" I got up and kissed her. I knew she would fix things. She always did. She reached out and grabbed my arm then. "What about you?" she said. And she peered up at me.

I asked her what she meant. She said, you know. When are you going, she says to me. I told her I'm not old enough yet.

"You soon will be, Harriet Hemings," she said to me. "You mama say you doan wanna go, either. What you so worried 'bout Beverly for when you doan wanna go yourself?"

His time is come, I told her. It's past due. And mine isn't here yet.

She chuckled then. "If you seed what your mama got up in her room, you wouldn't say that."

Well, I perked up then. She hardly ever leaves her little house, but I had no doubts that she knew if Mama had something up in her room concerning my leaving. She knows every secret on this place.

She chuckled more. Maddening. What does she have, I ask.

She shook her head. "Dresses," she chanted in that musical storytelling tone of hers. "Shawls, stockin's, boots, cambric underthings. Petticoats, gloves. You wanna hear more, Harriet Hemings?"

"What for?" I demanded. "Why does she have these things?"

"For you. When you leave."

Oh! I sank back down. The treachery! Oh! So now,

57

the final hurt. Mama's been sewing up a whole wardrobe for me, and I didn't even know it. Behind my back! Without even a by-your-leave. My own mother!

"You doan believe me?" Mammy asked. "Go up there to that little secret room she's got and see."

"I can't do that. I can't go up there."

"Oh? And why not, missy?"

"Because you can't get up there without going through the master's bedroom. And I'm not allowed in there. Nobody is."

She laughed, real low and cunning like. "Your mama stands guard over that room all day? She got nuthin' else to do?"

I said nothing. She was too smart for me, this old woman.

"Seems to me ifin I heard my mama was sewin' such things, I'd want to see for myself," she said. Then she got up. She's very heavy, and getting up she is cumbersome as a hogshead of coffee. So I helped her. She walked across the floor of her cabin to a shelf over the hearth. I saw her reach for a small sack made out of faded blue-and-white-striped cloth. From an old stone jar she took a few pinches of dry powder and put it into the sack. Then she handed it to me.

What's in it, I asked her. Oh, I was almost afraid to ask.

She smiled sweetly. "Good voodoo. Fresh cow dung mixed with red pepper and white people's hair, cooked over the fire and scorched 'til it could be ground into snuff. You sprinkle it around you when you go through the master's bedroom, and nobody will follow you.

58

And you'll come to no harm. Sprinkle some in the hall outside, too."

I nodded. I knew full well that if Mama ever caught me sprinkling anything on the immaculate floors of Monticello, she would box my ears good. But I couldn't hurt Mammy's feelings. So I thanked her.

"You go see for yourself what your mama is preparin' for you," she said. "And you better think, Harriet Hemings. And prepare yourself. Inside your head." And she tapped her temple.

Then she came closer and put her hand under my chin. "Long time ago, when your mama wuz younger then you is now, they had to ship Master Jefferson's youngest off to France. He wuz there and he wanted little Polly there wif him. But they needed somebody to go wif Polly on the ship. A black servant."

I'd heard the story so many times, but I said nothing.

She sighed. "They wanted to send young Sally Hemings. She wuz fifteen. They asked me. I said no, doan send her. But they doan listen to me. Her own mama, Betty Hemings, send her. You know why, Harriet Hemings?"

I said no, I didn't.

"Her mama figured when Sally got to Paris, she would see what it wuz lak to be free. And she'd stay. Her own mama wuz willin' to make that sacrifice, to never see her Sally agin. So she could be free."

Again she sighed, remembering. "But she doan stay. She come back wif her brother James. To Monticello. Now your mama wants you to have the chance she wuz too stupid to take."

I felt tears in my eyes. "You think Master Jefferson is my daddy, Mammy?"

And she looked at me with eyes so old it spooked me. "Not for me to say. For your mama."

"Mama won't talk about it."

"Your mama's the only one who kin talk 'bout it. Anybody else mouthin' off 'bout it, you might as well be listenin' to B'rer Rabbit."

"But you've been here! You've heard things."

"Only thing I hear worth repeatin' is that when Tom run, nobody stopped him. When Tom run, the master feel bad, but he set nobody out after him. That ought to tell you sumpthin', Harriet Hemings."

"The master don't want us to go, Mammy. And if I go, I'll have to run, too."

"Then run, girl. For all you're worth."

"You want me to leave, Mammy?"

"Chile, I'd sooner tear the eyes outa my head. 'Ceptin' I knows you have a chance to be free. And you gotta take that chance. For every nigra woman who doan have it. Same's your brother gots to do it for every nigra man."

I nodded my head. "Why did my mama not take her chance? Why did she come back?"

"You knows the answer to that same's I does. For him. The master. For love. She came back to live with B'rer Fox, 'cause she loved him. Now you git on wif you, Harriet Hemings. I gots to polish my pot." And she patted my arm. "All these years I tole you and your brother 'bout B'rer Rabbit and B'rer Wolf and B'rer Fox. Didn't you learn, chile? The both of you is

60

so stubborn. The both of you is lettin' B'rer Fox cook you over his fire."

"Master Jefferson isn't cooking me over any fire, Mammy."

"Thas how much you know. You is already stewed. Git along wif you. I gots to polish my pot."

I kissed her and left. The pot sat across the room on the hearth. It was made of cast iron, and she would take it to the song and preaching meeting later this afternoon. On some plantations, such meetings are forbidden, and such pots are used to capture the sounds of the meeting so white patrollers won't hear them.

But there are no white patrollers on or around Monticello. The master has no fear that his servants' meetings will encourage revolt. He has no qualms about them listening to black preachers, either. Doesn't Mammy realize that?

I allowed that she didn't. The woman whose job it is to tell nigra children stories of B'rer Rabbit and B'rer Wolf so they will have courage always takes along her pot. Just to be sure.

61

April 1820

A week has gone by, and I have not written in my journal. I had to wait a week before I got the chance to sneak into my mama's secret room. The following Sabbath, I finally got up there.

The house was very quiet. The master had taken Martha and her children and gone to pay calls down the mountain. My own mama was on Mulberry Row, where a nigra servant was birthing.

And so this afternoon I made my way into the master's sanctum sanctorum again. I got inside all right. And once in, I was determined to make the most of it. But this time, those rooms seemed spooked to me. I knew, in a minute, what it was, of course.

I could feel the master's presence all around me. Mammy Ursula would say it was his spirit in and around all his things.

Well, Harriet Hemings, I told myself, stop lollygagging and get busy. You have work to do. You could stand here forever and wish yourself a fine lady, but there isn't time.

So I crept past the master's bed to the door at the foot of it. Opening it I found a small stairway. It wound up and over the bed. I climbed.

With every step my heart jumped inside me like B'rer Rabbit being chased by B'rer Fox. When I reached the top, I just stood there with my mouth open. Like a jackass in the rain.

Because there it was. All of it. Just like Mammy Ursula had said. My observations hold good. And I will write it all down here before I forget.

First, that room is small and in the shape of what Mr. Oglesby would call octagonal. At the end are three round windows that look out on the mountains. Oh, it was like being in a bird's nest!

It is sparsely furnished. There is a small clothespress in the far corner, a stand with a washbasin and pitcher, and a small copper bathing tub that gleams. Linen towels are carefully laid over its rim.

Next to the bed is my mama's sewing basket. A clock, delicate and graceful, ticks on a small table.

Everything in the room speaks of my mama. Fragile. But strong.

But the clothes! Now, I am not one to hold with the belief that fine feathers make fine birds. But I was truly edified by that display of clothing.

I saw two chemises, right off. White and soft they were. There were petticoats of the softest cotton, dresses of lightweight wool — one of velvet!

The velvet was deep burnished gold in color. There

was a warm woolen cloak and an array of finely stitched underthings. I picked up a pair of stays. The color was deep forest green and the whalebone was not all stitched in yet.

Oh, how Mama must have pricked her fingers sewing in that whalebone!

There were even shoes. One pair was of a soft blue suede. I know the material because Martha Randolph has a pair just like them.

I held one blue shoe close to my breast. I had never had such elegant things, surely. Where had Mama gotten the fabric for such lovely clothes? The woolen cloak was lined with silk. The velvet of the dress was of a quality I had seen only on fine white ladies.

I sank to the floor. I was feeling wretched and probably could have used one of Mammy Ursula's concoctions. Oh, how I hated my mama for what she'd done here! And yet, at the same time, I loved her so much for all the trouble she'd gone through that I didn't know why I was crying.

It wore me out, all that crying. And then I must have dozed, sitting on the floor by Mama's bed.

"What are you doing here?"

The voice came to me like in a dream. It was part of my dream, and in that dream I was running after Beverly, who was chasing his balloon. At the far end of the field stood Thomas Jefferson, waiting for us.

"Harriet Hemings, I said what are you doing here?"

I came awake then, all right. Because of my position on the floor the first thing I saw was the man's boots. Then I raised my eyes, and there was the man himself.

64

It was getting dark in the room. But I could make out, plain as a toothache, that Thomas Jefferson was standing in front of me. And staring down. His bushy eyebrows were scowling. His face was very ruddy with anger.

I stared up at him. This is the man, I thought to myself, that Beverly says is my daddy. But I felt no affection for him in that moment. And I suppose he felt even less for me.

Then I determined that while the voice was stern and the features feigned anger, there was a light in his eyes. I would best describe it here as amusement.

I brushed my eyes and stumbled to my feet. "I just came up to — "

"You came up through my private quarters."

"Yes, Master . . ." My bones were turning to mush, like so much hominy. I started to tremble. ". . . but I didn't look at anything, Master," I said quickly.

The scowl was making furrows on his high brow. And the corners of his mouth were turned down. But the light in his eyes was still kindly.

"Did you walk through my quarters with your eyes closed, then?"

At first I did not understand. Then, understanding, I realized how foolish I sounded. "No, Master," I said. I was quite miserable.

"Then don't say you didn't look at anything. For I'm sure you did. That's what you came for, isn't it? To look? Well? Speak the truth."

I clutched the blue shoe to me and nodded. But I could not speak. "I didn't," I said.

"What? Speak up."

Oh, why didn't he just strike me and get it over with? But no, I thought, coming to my senses. Thomas Jefferson would never strike a slave. And I was still that, in spite of all his past kindnesses.

I tried to stand straight, as Beverly had done. I tried to look at him. I did for a moment, anyway. And what I saw there will remain with me forever.

There was tranquility in those blue eyes. And peace. But there was something else, too. I could not name it then, but I name it now.

Wisdom. It terrified me, that wisdom. And I know, thinking on it, that the wisdom in those eyes allows the peace to dwell in them, too. But there was sadness, also, when he looked at me. As if all his peace and wisdom had been purchased at a heavy price.

I became very decorous then. I curtsied. "I said, Master, that I didn't come to look at your things. And I touched nothing. I came up here. To see all this."

He nodded then. He looked around the room, and his eyes grew sadder, if that was possible. And I could see that he understood what he saw there. He reached out a hand to me for the dainty boot. I gave it to him. He turned it over and over in his hands.

"Your mama has been very busy up here," he said softly. "This is the room she uses when she cares for my wardrobe."

"Yes, Master." And, oh, I was grateful for the lie. I was happy to be part of it.

"Now I see she's sewing all kinds of woman's frippery up here. Who do you suppose these things are for?"

Then he fixed those blue eyes on me. Oh, Lordy, I prayed, I cannot hurt this man. He thinks he can hold on to what is his by love. With everything he knows, with all his books and ledgers, hasn't he learned yet that he cannot do that?

"I could not even venture a guess, Master."

A smile played about the corners of his mouth. I love it when he smiles at me. The blue eyes twinkled. And I knew, oh, Lordy I knew, that I was lost. For this man uses innocence as a weapon. He uses silence as a shield. He rules by kindness. And I just melted like beeswax in his presence.

"Well," and he is standing there contemplating that blue shoe like the good of his soul depended upon it. "I'm sure the person your mama is sewing for will never have worn such beautiful clothes. Sally Hemings puts love into whatever she does. Perhaps these clothes are for my granddaughter Ellen."

"Yes, Master." Ellen Wayles Randolph is twenty-four now and still not married. Or even betrothed. Her mother, Martha, calls her the jewel of her grandfather's soul. Yes, the jewel must be constantly kept in new clothes since she was always making romantic conquests.

"I'm sure they're for Miss Ellen, Master," I said.

He nodded. And he's satisfied with the lie. "But you shouldn't be here, nevertheless," he says sternly. "Not even to look. What would your mama say if she knew you were poking amongst her things?"

"She'd box my ears, Master." I summoned forth my most contrite expression, for I was sure that was what he wanted.

"Well, then, we mustn't tell her, must we?"

"No, Master."

"Come along, then, come along." He turned to go, and I followed him down the small winding staircase, noting how he had to stoop and hunch his shoulders to fit in the narrow passageway.

Downstairs he gestured I should follow, and I did so. At the door of his private quarters he looked down at me. "I shall keep your secret, Harriet Hemings, if you keep mine."

"What secret is that master?"

"I shall not tell anyone you were in here. If you promise not to tell that I caught you and did not punish you. It would diminish my authority. We can't have that now, can we?"

"No, Master."

"Fine. We understand each other, then. And you will forget what you saw up there today also. Won't you?"

Tears came to my eyes. He was asking me not to leave. He was asking me to forget that my mama was sewing a wardrobe for my departure. He was asking me to ignore all the evidence. And he was asking me to bide by his rule, which dismissed, by silence, anything unpleasant in the household. He wanted me to pretend my mother's efforts never took place. The way he responded over the years, with silence and pretense, to the savage rumors in the press about himself and Sally Hemings.

"Yes, Master," I whispered. I would do anything for him. I was under his spell.

He nodded his head, pleased. "Are you happy here at Monticello? Is your tutor kind to you? Do you always have enough to eat and are you warm and secure at night?"

"Yes, Master."

"Has anyone treated you badly? Do they work you too hard in the weaver's cottage?"

"No, Master."

"Good, good. I won't have anyone mistreating you. If anyone does, you are to come and tell me immediately. Do you understand?"

I nodded yes.

"And when you see that I am not too busy someday, come, and I will show you my seed closet. You like flowers. I've noticed you often wandering in the gardens and talking with Thruston. He collects the seeds for me, and I put them in phials on hooks and label them. Have you noticed how beautiful the dogwood and lilac are this year?"

I nodded. For I could not speak for the fullness in my heart.

"Thruston is one of the best men with flowers that I have known in my lifetime. Of course," and he bent low to confide in me, "the energies of the earth are a gift of nature. And any kind of gardening is a passion of mine. I see you have made Thruston one of your friends. I observe you often together."

I looked up to see his bemused expression. He was smiling slightly. And I know I blushed. "We grew up together, Master," I said.

"Yes, that you did. Well, old friends are the dearest. Eight years ago I started corresponding with my old friend, John Adams, after years of silence on both our parts. His letters are a constant source of joy to me. But Harriet . . ." He cleared his throat. ". . . to pursue this matter further, you and Thruston seem to take . . . shall I say, particular delight in each other's company, do you not?"

Oh, to think! To think he cared enough about me to inquire if what I felt for Thruston was more than friendship! Oh, he was so solicitous!

"We are just friends, Master," I said.

He nodded. For a moment, neither of us could think of what to say. Then I had a thought and brightened.

"I heard the whippoorwill this morning," I informed him.

This gave him pleasure. "Did you? I must record it in my Farm Book."

"And I noted, Master, that the tick has been out since March fifteenth."

He nodded solemnly. "Be careful when you run in the fields with your brothers, lest the tick bite you. I am sure your mother also cautioned you to be careful whenever you run about the fields and woods alone, hasn't she?"

His blue eyes were steady and kind. And in their depths I saw what must be fatherly concern. "I'm careful, Master."

"Are you writing in the journal I gave you?"

"Oh, yes, Master."

"Good, good. It is difficult for me to believe you are almost a grown woman, Harriet. Do you remember what you told your mother, as a child, when she sent you out from underfoot to play?"

I was startled then. I was caught unawares. No, I did not remember.

His smile was sad. He clasped his hands behind him and raised his eyes to the ceiling. " 'If God comes by when I'm out,' you would say to her, 'tell Him to wait. There are things I must ask Him.' "

I blushed then, and looked at the floor. I had completely forgotten my childhood game. It pleasured me that he should remember.

"I was always curious, Harriet. What was it you wanted to ask God?"

"The animals," I said. "I wanted to ask Him about the animals. And why He made them so different. I used to wonder . . ." But then I faltered, fearful he would laugh at me.

"Go on," he directed kindly.

"I used to wonder why God would ever make anything that looked like a pig. Such a big animal with those tiny ears and that little curled-up tail. And then how He could go and make anything as beautiful as a horse. And my brother . . ." Again I stopped, sure I would offend him.

But he wanted me to continue.

". . . my brother Tom would show me some books with drawings of other animals. He got the books from your library. Animals that were in far-off lands. He showed me drawings of elephants. And tigers. And the tall animal with the long neck."

"Giraffes," Thomas Jefferson said.

"Yes, that's the one. I wanted to ask God what He was thinking of when he made so many strange shapes and sizes and colors."

"Elephants, tigers, and giraffes," he mused. "Yes, I see your reasoning. You wanted to know what God had in mind when He made so many variations of the beast."

I breathed easy. He understood!

"Sometimes, Harriet, when I study human beings, when I ponder the fact that God made some white and some black and others Indian and yet others Chinese, I wonder what He had in mind, too. But I don't think it is ours to know. This God you always thought you would miss if He stopped by when you were out playing . . . I think I'd like to ask Him a few questions myself."

"You, Master?" I could not believe it.

"Ah, yes, Harriet. I have many questions. Many, child." He opened the door. "The older I get and the more I ponder the way of things, the more questions I have. You must run along now. Quickly." He stepped out into the hall. "I was glad for this chance to speak to you. But next time you wish to speak to me, you must seek me out in the parlor. Or on the grounds. You must not come in here again."

"Yes, Master."

"Be careful where you go. Or even think of going in your life. Give careful thought beforehand, and there will be fewer regrets later."

What was he saying? To give much thought before I decided to leave Monticello? I curtsied again, and he nodded in approval.

Oh, I wanted to throw my arms around him and tell him I would never leave Monticello, that there

72

was no reason for his concern. But I could not, of course. All I could do was walk away.

I almost danced down the hallway. He had spoken to me as if I were somebody! He had taken the time to inquire about my welfare! He had listened to what I had to say! I am not just another of his servants to him.

I am a person in my own right. With feelings. Oh, if I live to be as old as Mammy Ursula, I will never forget this conversation with Thomas Jefferson. My heart leaps inside me, thinking on it.

He talked with me as if he were truly my father.

The Middle of May 1820

I have not written a line in this journal for a fortnight now, and I scarcely know where to start. It has been a fortnight to try the soul of the most patient of us around here. And I am not on that list.

First, Mister Charles Bankhead himself came back. He's the one who beats his wife, the master's granddaughter Anne.

Well, after he stabbed Master Thomas Jefferson Randolph, Anne's brother, he never was brought to trial. Seems to me most white folk can get away with anything they have a mind to do. Any mischief, no matter how evil. This isn't the first time Bankhead has been offered hospitality here since that incident, either. I don't know why the master feels he has to open his house to him. But, when I ponder on how he opens this place to everybody this side of the Mississippi River who can make it up the mountain, I understand somewhat.

But Bankhead! He's no-count. Anne's own sister, Ellen Randolph, calls him a worthless drunkard. Never mind. Here he comes to supper about a week ago with Anne, acting like they were the most agreeable couple in Albemarle County.

Thomas Mann Randolph, Anne's father, was a dinner guest, too. The one and the same who tried to convince me to get my freedom a while back in our dining room conversation. And William Thornton and Benjamin Latrobe, who had helped the master draw up plans for his university, were there, also.

The kitchen was in a flurry all day. Such times my mama oversees the cooking. She was worried about Bankhead getting at the wine, and made sure that Burwell would refuse Bankhead brandy when he asked for it. Burwell keeps the keys to the liquor cellar.

All we needed, Mama said, was Bankhead in his cups and disgracing the master in front of Mister Thornton and Mister Latrobe.

Even I helped some in the kitchen. But I had a headache that had started in the weaver's cottage yesterday and never let up. So mama gave me a concoction with marjoram in it, since marjoram is for disorders of the head. And she made me sit in the kitchen and stop working, I felt so poorly. She heaped a plate full of tiny shrimp and roast pork seasoned with herbs and wild rice with mushrooms and pumpkin pudding.

I ate and fell asleep in the chair in the midst of all

the commotion, that's how worn out I was. Next thing I knew it was quiet. Dusk outside. The kitchen was empty. The air coming in the door was like silk. It's May now and the evenings are so lovely.

Thruston woke me. He was standing in the doorway, all gussied up in spotless sun-bleached breeches and a new homespun shirt.

"I brought some flowers," he says. And he comes in and shoves a bouquet of Sweet William at me. In his other hand is his fiddle.

You sure do look handsome, Thruston, I told him.

"Been playin' my fiddle for the party. Your mama and the others finished up here and tol' me to come get somethin' to eat."

I got up. I felt feverish and chilled at the same time. I showed him where the food was, in bowls and earthenware jars. He filled a dish of shrimp and pork and rice. He even took some turtle soup, though it was cold by now. He loaded his plate with greens and corn bread and sat on a low stool and commenced to eat.

How did they like your fiddle playing, I asked.

"Liked it fine. Master said it brought tears to his eyes."

"Mama told me the master dreams of having his gardeners and weavers and cabinetmakers all learning to play French horns and clarinets and other instruments so he can have a band of domestic musicians."

He wiped his mouth with the back of his hand. "Master's got big ideas for somebody who's in such debt."

"He isn't in debt. Who said so?"

"Mister Bacon said so. The master owes lots of money."

"Mama never said that."

"You hear only what you want to hear, Harriet Hemings."

"And you hear everything, I suppose."

"I hear more than you. And I doan even live in this house. I know 'bout the panic last year that closed so many banks in Virginia. I know the master sold all those slaves he sent over to his son-in-law. For money."

"You talking about the people he sent to Francis Eppes?"

"I is."

"Thomas Jefferson never sold a nigra servant in his life."

He chuckled. "He sold your mama's sister Thenia to James Monroe."

But I was quick as a fox with my answer. "Mister Monroe owned the father of her children. The master likes to keep families together."

"He didn't have to sell her. Could of given her away."

"Oh, Thruston! That was twenty years ago!"

He finished eating. "Well, he jus' sold more slaves. Needed money. Made hisself feel good by sayin' they is still in the family. But they is sold. And if'n he gets in more debt, you could be sold, too."

Well, I wasn't about to stand for that! "It's a lie!"

But he only chuckled again.

"Lie! I can never be sold! I'm free!"

"If you is free, what you doin' here in this kitchen lookin' like somethin' that wuz just dragged through the briar patch," he says.

"I'm sorry I don't look like a fine lady to you, Thruston. But I was helping Mama with the dinner party."

He said nothing then. Except that the flowers wanted water. So I got up and poured some into a bowl and arranged the flowers nicely. All the while I could feel his eyes on me, watching my every move, like a creature from the forest. What are you staring at, I asked him.

"A free nigger woman. Ain't never seen one before."

"You know it's so, Thruston. So does everybody else. Mama says I'm free when I'm twenty-one. If I want it. So is Beverly."

"You want it?"

"I haven't made my mind up, Thruston. But it's my mind to make up when I'm ready," I said.

He looked sad then, and if the truth be known, I felt satisfied. He had no right sashaying in here and telling me I was going to be sold.

"You wanna come walkin'?"

"I think not. I'm feeling poorly."

"Your mama say you've been actin' like a sick polecat these last couple of weeks."

So Mama had thought that I'd kept to myself the last few weeks since I found the clothes she was making for me, because I was sickly. Yes, I'd kept my distance from her. I just couldn't figure how to behave with her anymore. Sometimes I felt ornery towards her. Other times I loved her. It had me in such a state of agitation I was like a cat chasing its tail.

"A person can't have a headache and Mama's running down to Mammy Ursula for a potion for cholera," I said. "Mama's seen so many children die around here, every time I prick a finger it spooks her."

"You ain't no chile no more, Harriet Hemings."

Well, something in the way he said that made me pay extra mind. And sure enough, he was looking at me like a forest creature again. Next thing you know, he's standing real close and taking my hand.

"Don't," I said.

Why, he wanted to know. "You're kinda high and mighty these days. You never minded before when I held your hand."

I told him it was different now. He wanted to know why, but I wouldn't answer. Then he put his hands on my shoulders. "You too high and mighty fer a kiss?"

"I'm not high and mighty. But I'm not kissing you, either."

He chuckles again. "You is very high and mighty, Harriet Hemings. But you won't be that way for long."

I pulled away from him. "What do you mean?"

He laughs again. "Would you rather kiss Isabel's Davie?"

"Tell me what you mean, Thruston!"

He looked at me and there was, just for a minute, a streak so mean in him it was like a white line down a skunk's back. "Isabel's Davie got his eye on you. Tell me you doan know that. Every nigra servant under thirty-five has got his eye on you."

"There's plenty of other girls on Monticello for them to have their eyes on."

"Sure. And you think you is better than all those other girls. 'Cause you live up here in the big house. And 'cause your skin is light. Miss High and Mighty."

"That isn't true, Thruston and you know it. Don't talk about my light skin. It isn't fair. I can't help the color of my skin. And I'm not high and mighty. And you know that, too."

"Yeah, but they doan know it. And they is waitin' to take you down a peg or two. Isabel's Davie even says that's what he's gonna do, first chance he gets."

"Well, he's not going to get the chance."

He took my hand and pulled me closer. I wasn't worried. This was Thruston. I'd shoved his face in the dirt when I was four.

"He says he's gonna marry you."

"Marry! Ha!"

"Maybe you ain't noticed the way he been lookin' at you lately."

"I've noticed. And I'd never marry an animal like him. I'll never marry anybody who looks at me like that."

His hand tightened on my wrist. "Mister Bacon doan cotton to you sashayin' 'round here on the loose, lookin' like you do. Only means trouble for him."

Mister Bacon is the overseer. "He can like or dislike whatever he wants. I won't marry until I'm ready."

"When will that be?" he asked.

"Probably not until I'm twenty-one."

And, oh, his eyes got round and filled with distress. "If you doan plan on takin' that freedom of yours and leavin' when you're twenty-one, then you better start thinkin' 'bout what stayin' means."

"What does it mean, Thruston?"

He didn't answer for a minute. Then he said it, real low. "If you stay, you gotta marry."

"There's nobody to marry."

He was examining the flowers I'd put in a bowl. He was not looking at me. "Marry me," he said.

I felt so sad when he said that. No! I wanted to scream at him. No! Don't say it! We can't, Thruston. Can't you see how it all would end? But instead, I yelled at him. "I'd sooner marry a porcupine!"

He looked at me and I could see the pain in his eyes. And, oh, I felt so confused I wanted to sink right down on that brick floor and die. "Don't you see, Thruston?" I took a step toward him. He backed away.

"What can it mean for us? A cabin on Mulberry Row and more babies than Martha Randolph? At least she has servants to care for hers!"

"That's your fate if you stay, girl," he said. "There ain't nuthin' else. I doan care how white your skin is. What else is there?"

"I don't know, Thruston. Up until a few weeks ago when everybody started yapping at me about leaving, I just figured on living here forever. And us being friends. Like it's always been."

"It can't be that way no more," he said. "I tol' you,

81

Master's gettin' old. Gonna die soon. They'll want to marry you off soon. Your mama gonna marry you to Isabel's Davie if'n you doan marry me."

"I'd die before I'd marry Isabel's Davie. I'd put a knife in my heart! Why can't we just let everything go on, Thruston. A little while longer?"

"Doan say that 'bout puttin' a knife in your heart," he says sadly. "You gotta face the way things be. Master is seventy-seven. How long you figure he gonna live? He be dyin' one of these days. You think all this will go on? With me plantin' flowers and playin' the fiddle and your mama runnin' the house? Mister Bacon says the place'd be sold to pay the master's debts. A bidder will come."

"No!" I yelled it.

"Yes!" He shouted at me. "A bidder will come. Put us on the block. For sale. 'What'll I get for this fine nigra gal? She has quality.' They'll sell us all. And a white man would pay a good price for a piece of property like you."

"Stop it!"

He grabbed my arm. "You is a fool, Harriet Hemings."

"Why. 'Cause I won't marry you?"

"No. 'Cause you won't take your freedom. I want to marry you. You have to be crazier than a locked-up coon dog at huntin' time not to see it. But I'se tellin' you to take your freedom."

I am ashamed to say it, but I tried to slap him. Dear Thruston. My friend. He kept a hold on me, though, and went right on mouthing off.

"Why you think your mama wants you to leave? Thomas Jefferson doan even manage this place anymore. That grandson of his — Thomas Jefferson Randolph — does. And he ain't doin' so good at managin' from what I hears. You'd be a fool, Harriet Hemings, for not leavin'. Almost as much as a fool as you'd be for marryin' me."

"Well, those are the first true words that's passed your lips all night!"

He let me go. I rubbed my wrist, for it was chaffed. He walked to the door. "Some white man's gonna come along when the master dies and he's gonna have his way with you, Harriet Hemings."

"I'll be free if the master dies," I said.

"You think that?"

"Yes. Master made my mama that promise. So stop your fussing, Thruston. Me and my brothers will all be free."

"Ain't nobody gonna hold to that promise if'n the master dies. Ain't no white man gonna care 'bout no promise. Nobody gonna do right by it."

I was trembling now. My headache had returned. The top of my head felt as if someone had buried an axe in it. "I don't have to stand here and listen to any more lies," I said.

"They ain't lies, girl. They's the truth. But you doan like to face the truth."

"Lies!" And then I pulled the flowers out of the bowl and threw them at him. They hit him in the face. "You get out of here, Thruston." Oh, I was crying then. "You get out of here and leave me be!"

He just stood there in that doorway. The night had gotten dark behind him. Crickets were chirping like their fool lives depended on it. And he looked at me. "I'm goin'," he says, "Doan worry."

Then he turned and ran off into the night.

Mid-May 1820
That same night

Mammy Ursula is fond of saying that you don't speak some words, lest they take a life of their own and come back to spook you. Well, Thruston's words did just that, it seems. Though I know my dear friend would have put a knife in his own heart rather than think that any words that got past his lips caused bad things to happen to me.

It pains me just to recall what happened that very night after he left the kitchen. But I promised myself I would mark the truth in this book. And not some words dressed up in plumes and feathers to make right what never was.

So here is what happened. The house was empty once darkness fell. I suppose that if I pondered on it at all, I understood that the master and his guests were out walking the grounds. I don't know what I pondered after Thruston and I had our set-to. I was so distressed.

And when I get distressed, I walk around a lot. Just walking in this house comforts me, I love it so. I take strength from every object I see, and the sound of my own feet on the floors reassures me.

So I walked. Through all the downstairs rooms. I met Burwell, who told me the servants had gone back to Mulberry Row and my mama was upstairs resting.

Oh, my head ached so. I had to find Mama. But all I could think of was what Thruston had said about the master being in debt and me being sold.

The next thing I knew, I was in the dining room. The remains of the meal had been cleared away. Candles burned low on the table. How could Thomas Jefferson be in debt? Lordy, I thought, Thruston must be lying. Good thing I'd thrown those flowers at him. Next time I'd throw something better.

I was standing in front of the double glass doors, looking into the tearoom, no more aware of what I was about than a firefly, when I heard footsteps behind me. I turned.

At the other end of the dining room are two doors, one on either side of the fireplace. The door on the left goes to the entrance hall, the one on the right to the parlor.

The door to the parlor opened, and there stood Mister Charles Bankhead.

I felt myself go stiff and then limp. He peered at me across the polished table, on which were four huge candlesticks.

"Come for some brandy. That damned Burwell thinks he owns the place. Who's there? Ah," he came toward me. I could see he had already consumed as much brandy as he could and still be standing on his feet.

If that's what he was doing. He was giving a good imitation of it.

His frock coat was off and his cravat askew. His hair was rumpled, as if he had just awoken. "So, little missy," he says, "you know where the brandy is kept?"

I told him no, sir, I didn't. He'd have to see Burwell.

"Burwell!" he says. "Damned uppity darkie. Thinks he owns the place. All you darkies are too uppity." And his eyes go over me then, taking me all in. "Won't give out the brandy. Well, I'll find some." He starts looking around the dining room. And I tried to slither around and get out.

"Here, where you going? Harriet, isn't it? My, my, you sure have grown up, Harriet. Sally Hemings' little girl."

He started toward me. "Yes, yes," he said. "No more little girl. Well, maybe what I don't need is brandy after all. Maybe something else will substitute. They can have their damned brandy."

Next thing I knew, he was in front of me. "My, you're a fancy, aren't you, Miss Harriet? Where's that mama of yours been keeping you, anyway?"

"Please, Mr. Bankhead," and I tried to step aside. But he grabbed my wrist. "Where you going, my pretty?"

"To bed. I have a headache."

"So have I. So let's comfort each other, then."

He was so close to me I could smell the brandy on his breath. And, oh, it did smell evil.

Now I had sworn that if this Mister Bankhead ever

came at me like he was doing now, I'd kill him. But there I was, trapped. With nothing to protect myself. If I could get to the dining room table, I told myself, I'd pick up one of those solid silver candlesticks and hit him with it. I was moving in that direction, but he still had my wrist and was blocking my path.

Then he kissed me.

I don't know what kisses are supposed to be like. Oh, I'd heard enough talk on Mulberry Row. But his was angry and brutal. I tried to free myself. But he was gripping my shoulders, and I felt like a trapped animal.

He smelled of liquor and his breath was sour and I tried to scream. I beat at his shoulders with my fists. His kiss was so vile and ugly I thought I would die.

Then he finished. "What's the matter, Harriet? You don't like being kissed?"

I tried to slap him, but he grabbed my wrist and called me a foul name. "You raise your hand to a white man? You darkies around here need to be put in your place!"

"Let me go," I said. I struggled, but he pulled me toward him again. And there, in that very genteel dining room, he put his hands on me.

I could not scream. His mouth was on mine. I felt fear close in on me. I felt disgust like a knife in my heart. His hands were all over me, under my petticoat, doing things I had heard about only in whispers on Mulberry Row.

I fought. Oh, how I fought! Anger and fear gave me strength. I kicked. Oh, how I wish I had sturdier shoes on my feet. I scratched, because he couldn't control both my hands. I pulled his hair.

His body was pressing on mine. I screamed out even though my scream was stifled. He was pushing me to the floor. Oh, this wasn't happening to me! How could it be happening here, right here inside this house that I love? Inside this genteel dining room?

He moved his mouth off mine, to breathe, I suppose. And I cried out. Then his hand came down over my mouth and his face was above me. I was on the floor. "You scream again, wench, and you'll feel my hand across your face. Now you just hush, girl, I'm gonna teach you a lesson."

"Let go that girl. You there!"

Someone, oh, someone was mercifully here. My head was pounding, and I was breaking out into a cold sweat.

"I said let her go!"

Thruston! Where had he come from? Never mind; he was there, pulling Bankhead off me. They were scuffling now. Bankhead was unsteady on his feet and swung at Thruston. In the dusk I saw them, two figures facing each other as if in a minuet.

I sat up on the floor. "You hurt, Harriet?" Thruston asked.

"No. I'm all right." My head felt like Mammy's pot being drummed on. I grasped the table and stood up.

"So, darkie," Bankhead said to Thruston, "you'd hit me, would you?"

Though my head was throbbing, I saw Bankhead, by the fireplace now, pick up a poker. "No!" I screamed.

There were footsteps then, other people in the room. Burwell first. "Stop this!" Burwell ordered. He

89

may be old, but he is full of dignity. His hair is almost white. He stood between Thruston and Bankhead. "Put that down, Mister Bankhead," he said real calm like. "You don't want to use that poker now."

"I'll kill him," Bankhead said. He and Thruston were circling each other, Thruston ready, with clenched fists. Then Bankhead pushed Burwell out of the way. He did it with such force that Burwell hit the wall. I screamed again.

I don't know what would have happened then if another figure hadn't come into the room. It was so dark I couldn't make out at first who it was.

"What's going on here?"

Oh, it was Mister Randolph. Thomas Mann Randolph, the master's crazy son-in-law, who was governor of Virginia. Mister Randolph surveyed us all, me hugging myself and crying, Burwell dazed from being thrown against the wall, and Thruston and Bankhead like two dogs snarling at each other.

"God help us," Mister Randolph said. "Charles, give me that poker, you damned idiot."

It was then that I recollected that Bankhead was Mister Randolph's son-in-law. Oh, Lordy, we do have one mixed-up household here. I'm surprised we all haven't gone at each other with pokers before this.

Bankhead refused, of course. He let out a stream of profanity at his father-in-law, as I blush to recall but will not write down here.

"You! You'd defend these darkies against me! He attacked me!" And Bankhead pointed the poker at Thruston.

"Not true, Mister Randolph, suh," Burwell stepped

forward. "This drunken fool here, pardon me, suh, this man was forcing his attentions on Miss Harriet and Thruston tried to stop him."

"Harriet!" Then Mister Randolph's eyes were on me. "Are you all right, child?"

I was sobbing and gulping, but I nodded yes. "You crazy, drunken fool." And Mister Randolph went right at his son-in-law then, and grabbed the poker from him. But first Bankhead tried to hit him with it. Mister Randolph is stronger, however, and they wrestled for a minute with Thruston and Burwell just champing at the bit to get in on it, and Mister Randolph shouting them off. Mister Randolph got the poker then, and knocked his son-in-law down with it.

Bankhead fell to the floor, and his face was bleeding. Mister Randolph was breathing very hard. "Get Martha, Burwell," he said. "Quick. Tell her to bring some rags and some remedies. I've near killed this fool son-in-law of mine. If it had been a square blow, I would have."

"Yessir," said Burwell. Then Mister Randolph told him not to tell the master. And Burwell ran off.

"Get out of here, both of you," he said to me and Thruston.

"I'll stay, sir, and explain things if'n the master comes," Thruston said.

"Don't be a fool. Nothing to explain." Mister Randolph knelt over his son-in-law, who was saying that all he wanted was some brandy. That if they'd given him some brandy, this wouldn't have happened.

"Go, I said," Mister Randolph ordered Thruston.

Thruston looked at me, and I said I'm all right, and

he went out. For some reason I stayed. "Thank you, sir," I said to Mister Randolph.

"Did he harm you?"

"No, sir. He just tried. I fought him off."

"Good for you. Wish I'd killed him. He beats my daughter all the time. Go on with you, Harriet. Find your mama. Go to bed, child; you look like death."

I made a brief curtsy and left the room.

I lay trembling in my small bed and looking out the window up at the stars. Hot tears rolled out of the corners of my eyes. Outside my window those were the same stars I'd seen every night. How could they be the same, I wondered? My whole world had changed. How could they not have moved or fallen?

I hadn't gone to find my mama. I went out of my way not to see her, and undressed and crawled into my bed like a wounded animal. Oh, I needed one of Mama's potions, all right, but I wouldn't ask. I didn't want her to know what had happened to me. I didn't want anyone to know.

But Thruston knew. So did Burwell. And Mister Randolph. Would they tell the master now? Would Mama or Mister Bacon make me marry? Would the talk on the place be that I sashayed around, that I enticed Mister Bankhead? Like a common woman? A doxie on the street?

Surely they knew his reputation. Mister Randolph and Burwell and Thruston knew he'd been drinking.

I rolled over in bed, sobbing. What I couldn't bear was that this was just what Thruston had said would happen to me earlier this evening. Some white man would have his way with me if I didn't leave Monticello.

Oh, I couldn't bear Thruston knowing he was right. I couldn't stand the memory of Bankhead's hands all over me, under my dress. Of his evil-smelling mouth against mine.

My body felt bruised. My mind felt betrayed. My skin felt like it wanted to come off.

Someone came into the room then, bearing a candle. "Harriet!"

It was Mama. "Harriet, child."

She leaned over me, but I turned away. I turned my face to the wall. She sat next to the bed, saying nothing. And next thing I knew, there were cold rags on my head and I stopped sobbing. Then she was making me drink something and wash my mouth out. Then I was drinking again, and this time she was making me swallow.

In the dark I could see only her eyes, yellow with fear. "He harm you?"

"No, Mama, I fought him."

"You sleep, then. This will make you sleep. Drink more."

I was trembling so I couldn't hold the cup. She held it for me. I was babbling, too, about not wanting the master to know, of not wanting to marry and how I'd die before I'd marry Isabel's Davie.

"Nobody going to make you marry anybody, baby," Mama said.

"Don't tell the master," I pleaded. "I don't want him to know."

"You've got nothing to be ashamed of," Mama said.

She washed my face then, and gave me a soft pillow. I lay back. The potion was starting to work. I felt my arms and legs getting limp. I felt the pain in my head going away. And I was in some other place then, somewhere soft and protected. And safe.

I slept. Demons came into my dreams, and I cried out. But Mama was there. All night. When she spoke, the demons left. Then, finally, I knew blessed nothing at all.

May 1820
Two days later

Oh, Lordy, I slept. Couldn't get enough sleep, it seemed. Every time I heard a noise or footsteps in the room I tried to open my eyes, but they felt like I had flatirons on the lids. Too much bother, so why try? So I slept some more.

After a while, Mama's voice just worked its way into my head, like a bumblebee working its way into a flower. I tried to push that voice away, but she would have none of it. How you feeling today, she says, like I'm ready to get up and dance to Thruston's fiddle playing. I said I was tolerable. So then, she says, open your eyes.

So I tried again. And what did I get for all my trouble? They hurt so bad from the sunshine in the room, I felt like a skunk by daylight.

What day is this, I asked. Thursday, she says. You've slept two days. There was rain last night. Mister Randolph came in soaked again. Fool man almost drowned fording that river on his horse. At the mention of his name, of course, it all came back to me, and I wanted to just curl up and die. Get up, she says. I told her I didn't want to get up. Want to stay here, I told her. The days, they just bleed right into each other, and that suits me just fine.

Then she tells me I have to get up, that Mister Randolph has been inquiring about me, and since he came to my rescue, it was time I got up and thanked him. She's purring it, the way she does when she wants something out of me. So I said I would. I ought to know better than to trust Mama when she purrs like that, but somehow I just never learn.

I was done up in my good cotton petticoat, best muslin chemise, and a brand-new short gown. Blue. I sat on my bed and Mama braided my hair in back. Sunlight dappled the room. Outside everything was fresh and clean.

"You all right, child?" Mama asks for about the tenth time. I said yes, but I knew I was not. Everything seemed so new, so different, so changed. It looked as if the world were made of glass, only it was all broken in pieces. I saw a kaleidoscope once. A visitor brought one to Monticello shortly after they were invented a few years ago. The master allowed me to look into it. And I saw lots of jagged pieces of colored glass.

That's what the world looked like to me now. I wondered if I got up, would the floor hold. How could I trust anything?

"Is everybody talking about me, Mama?"

"People got other things to talk about," she says.

"You're not so important as you think."

"Did the master ask what happened?"

"I told him. He's banished Charles Bankhead for the summer. He would do it forever, he says, except that Bankhead is married to his granddaughter, and he can't punish Anne like that."

I asked her if the master thought I was to blame, and she tugged my braid until it hurt. Why should he, she asks. He knows better. Anyway, Thruston told him what happened. So did Burwell. And Mister Randolph. All he wants is that you be all right. He says you're to take a week off from the weaver's cottage and rest. And he wants to see you before the week is out. He'll let you know when."

I felt a rush of warmth. "I love Thomas Jefferson, Mama."

"He's a good man," she says quietly. "But it's Mister Randolph you're to see today. Soon as I finish this braid."

"Now I'll get a lecture," I said. "Like last time. You put him up to it last time, Mama. You put him up to something today, too?"

"I haven't," she says. "I swear to you."

I believed her. I can read Mama by the tones of her voice. And in truth, I felt no concern just then. I felt peaceful, cared for, as if things were being arranged behind my back to make things right for me again.

"Can I ask a question, Mama?"

"Hold your head still now. What is it?"

"Is Master Jefferson in debt?"

"Where did you hear that?" she asks. I told her from Thruston. So she tells me then.

"The wheat is selling this year for a third of what it once brought. Farms all over the country are being sold by sheriffs at heavy losses. A good horse can be bought for five dollars these days. Everybody is in debt."

"Is the master's debt very bad?"

"Debt is always bad."

"Is he going to be poor?"

"Why worry your head about that, child."

"Thurston said . . ."

But she only laughed. "He's more discouraged than poor these days."

"About what?"

"About the country. About the fight Congress carried on for three months earlier this year, the fools, over the admission of Missouri into the Union."

"Why is he sad about that?"

"He's worried about the country. There were eleven slave states and eleven free. Then Missouri wants to come in as slave. There were those who said it would tip the balance. So they fought. Finally they agreed to let Maine in as free to balance things out. It was the fighting that made him sad. He fears for the Union."

"Why?"

"He talks about an imaginary line they are drawing across the country, with certain states slave and others free. He says a hideous evil is dividing America. He says the line will never be erased. Some Southern states threatened to leave the Union if Missouri wasn't admitted as a slave state. He says it fills him with terror."

"Thruston says if the master dies, we could all be sold as slaves."

I waited. She tied a white ribbon at the end of my braid. Then she turned me around. Her eyes were like amber torches, like the light that pine torches give off in the dark. "Haven't I been talking and talking, until my mouth can't say any more words, about you taking your freedom when you get to be of age? What do you think I mean, girl?"

"But Mama," I whispered fearfully, "what if the master dies *before* I become of age? Is it true what Thruston says? Could I be sold?"

She sighed and folded her arms across her middle. She tightened her lips. "Who knows?" And her voice was dead like. "I trust no one. So go downstairs and see Mister Randolph. The time has come to talk plain, Harriet."

So she didn't know either, for all her closeness with the master. But it was the first time we had ever spoken of such a possibility, and somehow I felt it was the first time she had ever really been honest with me.

I went downstairs. I moved through rooms and halls as if under a spell. Then I saw Mister Randolph outside the east portico, strolling on the brick walk where it was embosomed in trees. I went outside and stood on the portico, and he saw me and raised a hand in a gesture of greeting. So I walked down to meet him.

My limbs were a little wobbly, but the morning was cool and washed by the sun, with everything looking fresh and clean after a good rain. And, under those trees, standing with Mister Randolph and looking back to the house, it was like bad things had never happened to me.

"How are you, Harriet?" he said.

I told him I was tolerable, thank you. He suggested we walk a bit. And so we did. Away from the house.

We walked across the lawns near some oval flower beds. "Bankhead never should have been allowed back here," he said. "The man has the morals of a leech."

I agreed.

"He's left here with my Anne. I should have killed him. I may, next time I hear that he's beaten her."

I said nothing. Such anger from this gentle and modest man surprised me. But I could not fault him for it. Although he did not live with his wife and younger children, I have heard he is greatly attached to all his sons and daughters.

"He should have been brought to trial when he stabbed my son. No one pushed for it. Because the disgrace would have hurt the family. I promised my father-in-law I'd give Bankhead another chance. That's why he was allowed back here. That, and because your master so loves Anne he can't bear not seeing her."

And then in the next breath he told me this: "You have to think about leaving here, Harriet." He said it plain and soft, like he was remarking about the weather.

And, plain and soft, like I was in complete harmony with him, like the soft sound of the wind against the sky, I said yes, sir, I know.

For I did know. Perhaps I had always known. But

one thing was certain. What Charles Bankhead had done to me, was the occasion for me to admit it. And what Mama had said to me just a little earlier, admitting I could be sold if the master dies before I reach twenty-one, didn't do any harm, either.

Now I was ready to talk about it.

"When will you be of age?" he asked.

I told him. May of 1822.

"Yes, of course," he said. As if he was supposed to know my age, this poor, dear man who has so many children of his own he can't even recollect all their names.

"Well," he said, "you should know that any freed slave must immediately leave Virginia. It is the law. Unless the owner secures special dispensation from the legislature. That rule was made in 1806. Have they told you of it?"

I said no, they hadn't.

He sighed. "Mister Jefferson will have to see that you are better educated before you leave. And I mean to tell him that. I mean to help you."

"Why?" I asked.

"For so many reasons, Harriet. All of which are like a confused jumble in my head. In part because I want to free all Virginia's slaves and know I won't be able to. In part because I should have killed Bankhead when he stabbed my son. Because I backed down from insisting he come to trial. Thus allowing him loose again upon the world.

"And because," he sighed again, "Bankhead represents everything that is so despicable about this system we live under. And I see you as a victim, along with my Anne. For the same system that nurtures slavery, nurtures and tolerates all the evil impulses in men. It tolerates their laziness. And violence. It looks the other way when they turn from their wives to the women in the quarters and produce children like you and your brothers, who are left to find their way in such confusion, belonging neither to the nigra nor the white community, yet being part of both."

I said nothing, though tears came to my eyes.

"Now I have a plan," he said. "And I will propose it to my father-in-law, and he will accept it and carry it out. Or the next time Bankhead strikes my Anne, I will surely end his life. And truly bring disgrace down upon this family."

I nodded. Everything he said I knew to be true. I could feel it in my bones. And I felt, too, the good voodoo there was between us, as Mammy would call it.

"First, you will meet with the master and tell him you intend to leave when you are of age. Before that I will approach him and tell him we have talked and you dearly wish to do this thing. I will suggest he allow my wife to school you in the domestic and gentle arts, so you can take your place in the world. Do you agree to that?"

I had the feeling that the world was breaking in two in front of me, changing right before my eyes. As if someone were shaking the kaleidoscope.

"If you do not agree, Harriet, and you do not take your freedom, they will marry you off. Your mother is of the mind that Mister Bacon will be wanting to marry you off when he hears of what happened the other night. Is it in your heart to marry one of Thomas Jefferson's slaves?"

"No," I said. I said it so plain he could not mistake my vehemence.

"If you have no one you care for, Mister Bacon will force the matter. He will pick someone for you."

"Isabel's Davie," I murmured.

He looked into my eyes. "I take it you don't want that."

"I'd die first."

"No dying, Harriet. You are too young and full of life. So then, you are prepared to make your decision to leave. We can go ahead."

I took a deep breath. "Will I be like Tom? Never to come back?"

He spoke gently. "Yes, I'm afraid so. But I think you have the courage to begin your life anew. What do you know of Tom?"

"Nothing. Mama never speaks of him to me."

"She should. It would give you courage if she told you."

"Told me what?"

"It's for her to say. I'll suggest to her that she do so."

For a moment my interest was stirred. Had they had news of Tom? But then my fears took over. "Can't the master get this special whatever it is, from the legislature?"

"Special dispensation? He won't do that. What reason would he give, child? Think on it. Special dispensation for the mulatto daughter of Sally Hemings? The woman they said, for years in the press, was his concubine? Don't you see what it would do to him? And your mother?"

I nodded yes, but I didn't see at all. The master had been President of the United States. Surely, as Beverly had said, he could do just about anything he wanted.

"No, you must leave Virginia," Mister Randolph insisted. "But I am afraid it is not that simple, Harriet. There is more to consider."

More? Wasn't all this enough?

"Mister Bacon could still take it in his head to marry you off. You are a young woman of fine appearance. It could cause him trouble he has no need of."

"I won't marry," I said. "They can't make me."

"There are two years yet until you come of age." He ruminated a bit. "It would help if you were betrothed, Harriet. It would protect you."

My eyes went wide. "How? There is no one here who would become betrothed to me if they knew I was leaving. They couldn't. They are all slaves. And I know no one away from this place."

"Ah, yes." He smiled. "But I do."

He smiled with such a luminous expression on his face that I became happy, too. Although I mark here that I knew he was up to something.

"I know many people," he said. "And I have much influence. But I sense I won't have to look too far afield. You have an admirer."

I stopped dead in my tracks. My hand flew to my chest. "You jest," I said.

But now his face was perfectly solemn. "I would not do that, Harriet. I respect you and your mama far too much."

"Who is this admirer?"

"A young man who has been here a few times over the years. To confer with the great Thomas Jefferson about architecture. A young architect who remarked, once or twice in my presence, about you and your brothers. He was greatly distressed by the lightness of your skin and how it suggested that you had so much white blood in you. Indeed, more white than nigra. He considers slavery a great moral evil to begin with, so he was horrified to see people who are as white as you and your brothers, kept as slaves."

Both my hands were across my heart. He went on.

"He holds you in high esteem."

"Who is this person?" I breathed.

"I only need suggest to him that you will soon be taking your freedom and leaving here. He never dreamed, when he spoke of you to me, in such admiring terms, that such a thing would someday happen. So he never dared form a thought in his mind concerning you. But I know him, Harriet. For his mind to take that next step, I need only tell him you will be free in the future."

I just stared at this man. He said the words with such kindness and yet with such shyness that I felt a genuine rush of affection for him. This dear, awkward man. They all say he is crazy. His wife refuses to live with him. I knew, because it is common gossip on the place, that he is dismal at managing money, that when they were first married Martha always complained about a shortage of funds and the master had given him several loans.

But do they ever consider how good and dear he is?

No. They all hold him in low esteem. Only my mama shows him any real kindness.

"But how will I meet this man?" I managed to say.

"That can be arranged. He'll be visiting again. Who is to say that when he does visit you can't come upon him in the gardens? Or that your mama won't ask you to serve him tea? For you must meet him and talk before you decide if the arrangement would be agreeable to you. Part of being free, Harriet, is standing on your own and making your own decisions. I told you this once before."

I nodded, comprehending.

Then he looked at the ground for all the world like he was going to talk to the flowers in the manner of Thruston.

"There is one consideration, Harriet," he said. And the way he said it made me look sharp.

"This man is white, of course. You understand that."

White. It was like a thunderclap in my ears. It took my breath away. Already feeling as weak as a pig with its throat cut, I became weaker. Surely he couldn't be serious!

He looked at me in a most contrite way then. "It is something you should consider, Harriet," he said. "Passing."

My mouth went dry. "Passing?"

"Oh, come, child. You have pondered on it, I'll wager. Why, if you take your freedom, I'd advise you to do it. It would make the difference between having a good life and struggling. In my mind there is no question. As a free nigra, restrictions will always be imposed on you. You'll always have to carry your free

106

papers, and they can't guarantee your safety in some places. So why not take the smooth passage for yourself and your children."

My children? And it came to me then what he meant. "Marry a white man and pretend to be white," I said dully.

"Yes, Harriet. You would have little trouble doing so."

"But, I would be giving up everything I am," I said slowly.

"Yes, Harriet. True. But what you are now is a slave. Do you find that so difficult to give up?"

I did not answer. My mind was all addled. I felt like B'rer Fox had me cornered in the briar patch. Whichever way I turned, I couldn't get out.

"This man who so admires me," I asked. "He would not take me as I am?"

"He is quite smitten with you as you are, Harriet, yes. And I know him well enough to understand that he would not want, ever, for you to truly give up what you are. But to live in the outside world we must conform to its vagaries and stupidities. If you decided this man was someone you could care for, I am sure you would want to protect him and yourself and any children from the onslaughts of public outcry."

"Oh," I murmured.

"He has a fine profession in Washington City, Harriet. He is much in the public eye. But all that is yet to be pondered. One step at a time. Believe me, you could accomplish this if you set your mind to it. You are quality, Harriet."

I murmured my thanks to him.

"Shall I speak to him, then?" he asked.

He was waiting for my acquiescence. I looked up to see him smiling eagerly at me. "But what of my people?" I said. "How can I live if I turn my back on them? On what I am?"

"What are you, Harriet?" he asked.

I cast my eyes up at him, miserably.

"You are mostly white, Harriet. On your mama's side your great-granddaddy and your granddaddy were both white."

"My great-grandma was full-blooded African," I said.

He nodded. He sighed. "I understand, Harriet," he said. "But then, if these people are yours," and he waved a hand in a sweeping gesture that took in the whole plantation, "why not consider that you can't help them as a nigra. But you can, perhaps, someday, as a white. I can say no more now, child. Perhaps you need time to think on it. It's all been too much for you, these past few days. You've been booted into the future by leaps and bounds."

Yes, time, that was it. I smiled weakly at him. But I was a child no longer. What had happened the other night had ended my childhood forever. It had put me face to face with a brick wall and nowhere to go. And this dear, kind, misunderstood man was forging a hole in that wall for me and attempting to lead me through it.

I curtsied. "Thank you, sir, for all your kindnesses. I will ponder on it, I promise."

"You have only a few days, Harriet. I must meet with your mama and Mister Jefferson. Within a few days he will be wanting to speak with you. You should tell him, then, that you wish to take your freedom. And he will, if I know Thomas Jefferson at all, arrange for you to start your lessons. But they will be of a much better quality if you tell him you wish to pass."

I nodded.

"My wife and my daughter, Ellen, have drawn up a list of books for their own reading. I find it differs little from the list Mister Jefferson compiled for male youths who came to him for help. I know he does not expect young ladies to pursue the works of technology or venture far into mathematics or natural philosophy, but I am sure he will want you to study this list of books, if you tell him you are passing. Even as my wife and daughter do."

"Yes, sir," I said again.

"Passing is for your own protection, Harriet. Becoming betrothed would insure that not only Mister Bacon, but all the nigra servants on this place leave you alone over the next two years."

"I understand," I said.

"They all say I am crazy, Harriet. Perhaps I am. Oh, don't protest. I know how they speak of me. But I also know that the world is such that it helps to be a bit mad. Do you trust me?"

"Oh, yes, Mister Randolph!"

"Good. Then I am sure you will come to the right decision. Your mama will inform me what that decision is. And if you decide to pass, I will contact your admirer. So," and he sighed. "It is done then, Harriet. On my part. I bid you farewell. For now."

He left me there on the brick walk. Alone and

confused. Yet less terrified than I had been. For I had someone to help me now. And the thought of leaving was no longer a sickness inside me.

Of course, the thought of passing was. But for Mister Randolph I would ponder on it.

The Third Week of May 1820

For the next few days, Mama insisted I take my ease. So I did. Lordy, I had enough to keep my mind buzzing like a bumblebee in June. But I felt less free to wander about the place as had been my custom. I stayed close to Mama as she went about her duties.

She was overseeing the bleaching out of the bed and table linens. After the linens were bleached, they were mended. We sat in the coolness of the underground kitchen doing this task. It was two days after I had met with Mister Randolph. And then, with such calm you would think she was remarking on the weather, Mama said I should just put down that bed sheet and take myself upstairs to the entrance hall, that the master wanted to see me.

I sat like a piece of petrified wood. "Oh, I can't, Mama, I can't," I said.

"And why can't you?"

In two days, though I'd stuck to her close as a burr to a dog's tail, she'd not asked me about my conversation with Mister Randolph. But I just knew he'd told her of it. They were such friends and I knew they confided in each other.

I commenced to cry then. I dropped the bed sheet and put my face in my hands and wept.

"Now, why are you crying, child? You don't like what Mister Randolph proposed to you?"

"You know, then," I sobbed.

"Of course."

"Why didn't you *tell* me! Oh, Mama, I've been so miserable, not knowing what to *do*!"

"I wanted to give you room to wander in your own thoughts," she said softly. She was sitting very near to me and our heads almost touched. She patted my brow with her cool, delicate hand. She stroked it. Oh, I couldn't bear it! I reached out for her and she wrapped her arms around me as I sobbed.

"Foolish child," she said. "You've been given a chance other nigra servants on this place would kill for, and you're crying."

I pulled away from her and wiped my nose with my apron. "I'm not crying because of taking my freedom, Mama. I aim to take my freedom when the time comes. I told Mister Randolph that."

"Then why are you crying?"

"You know, Mama! He wants me to pass as white!"

"Is that so bad?"

"Mama! How can I turn my back on my people?"

"Your brother Tom did."

"What?" I gaped at her. My mouth fell open. Tom?

What was she saying? And then I recollected what Mister Randolph had said. Something about urging my Mama to tell me about Tom. I stood up.

"You're telling me Tom passed as white?"

"Yes." She looked up at me, her amber eyes begging me to understand.

"*Why!*"

"So he could make it out there in the world," she said simply.

"I mean, why did you never tell me this before? Why do you never speak of Tom? Don't you think that Madison and Eston and I want to know what happened to him?"

She shook her head slowly. "Harriet, Harriet," she said sadly. Then slowly, with the motions of an old woman, she got to her feet so her eyes were level with mine. "What's the sense? He's gone."

"The sense?" I couldn't *believe* what she was saying! "The sense is that we just might want to know what happened to our brother! Why do you keep it from us?"

"Because there's nothing to tell," she said sadly.

"But you just said — "

"I just said he passed as white. I had a letter from him a few years back. Just one letter in all the years he's been gone. He's doing fine, he's married, he's made me a grandmother, and he's passed as white. He's married a white woman. That's all I know, Harriet, I swear to you."

My chin quivered as I contemplated her. There were tears in her eyes. She shook her head back and forth, trying to make the right words come out of her mouth.

"I can't speak of him, Harriet," she whispered. "Not to anybody."

And she turned away then and began to weep, quietly. I had never seen my mama weep. I did not know what to do. I went to her, stood by her, touched her. "I'm sorry, Mama," I said.

She nodded while she composed herself. Then she turned toward me and took one of my hands in both her own and spoke. "I never would have mentioned him to you, Harriet, but I thought you should know that he passed. In his note to me, he still sounded like my Tom."

"Does his wife know who he is?"

She shook her head. "Yes, I think so."

"Yet nobody else out there knows he comes from Monticello? And that he is Tom Hemings?"

"No," she said softly.

"But how can I do this, Mama? I could *never* do it! I couldn't bear people not knowing who I was! I'm proud of who I am, Mama! Surely, Tom is, too!"

"Inside him," she said, "he knows who he is. And that's what's important."

Well, that was just like my mama, to say such a thing. "And he just mixes in the white world and forgets all about his people? What about *that*, Mama?"

She took both my hands in her own then. "Who knows what his children will accomplish someday," she said to me. "And they will know who they are. And it will be because Tom has given them the chance."

I nodded. "And so you think I should do this, too, now? You think I should pass. Like Tom. And become

114

betrothed to this man Mister Randolph has in mind for me."

"Whether you become betrothed to this man or not is your affair," she said. "It would protect you for now, yes. When you leave here, you can marry him or not. But, oh, my child. My Harriet. If you never listen to me about another thing, listen to me about this passing. I was right about taking your freedom, wasn't I? I'm right about this too, child, I swear it."

"Oh, Mama!" I wailed.

"Oh, Harriet, this freedom is worth everything. There is no sacrifice too great. Knowing that Tom is free and out there and making it is the only thing that helps me bear the sorrow of hearing from him just once in all these years. And if you could pass and have a life of your own, never worrying about having your free papers on you or listening for someone to make you account for what you are about! Just like all those white folk in Thomas Jefferson's America! Oh, Harriet!"

I ran to her and threw my arms around her. I could not bear the look on her face, the stricken look, the appeal, the tears. For I loved her more than anything. She was my mama. And for her I would do it.

The master was standing in front of the wide folding doors that overlook the east balcony. He was standing underneath the seven-day calendar clock. Sunlight streamed in the windows, which measure from ceiling to floor. I saw him before he heard me. I was able to creep up on him, like some forest creature.

His back was to me. He was dressed in plain brown

breeches and coat. His hair, almost white now, was tied back in a perfect queue. He might be old, I thought, but he is still striking.

Then he turned and saw me and smiled. And my bones turned to mush. I had always been a little afraid of him. In his eyes, there is blue fire. When he tightens his lips it is as if he is making up his mind to allow the sun to shine. Oh, what would he say to me now when I told him I not only wanted my freedom, but that I wanted to pass!

I must be careful, I cautioned myself. Not to let him pull me into his spell. For then I will never leave here. I must keep in mind the feeling of Charles Bankhead's hands upon me. Always. And know that could be my future if I stayed.

"Good day, Harriet."

I curtsied. A few times when we'd come upon each other unexpectedly in the flower gardens he had looked at me as if he were trying to decide who I was and where I'd come from. He had that look on his face now.

"You are well now?" he asked.

I allowed that I was. Then he asked me to come and sit next to him. In front of the long windows were two wooden chairs with spindle backs. He sat down on one and patted the other.

I sat. What was the cause of my illness, he wanted to know.

"Your mother has determined it was not cholera, for which we are all grateful."

I was struck dumb. I know Mama had told him what Bankhead had done to me. I looked into his face. Oh, he knew, surely. I saw the sorrow in his blue eyes.

But he cannot bring himself to speak of it, I thought, so he is acting like he acted years ago when they accused him, in the press, of taking my mother for a mistress. He never spoke of it. And his accusers went away.

"I had fever and chills, Master," I said. "And my bones ached."

"You were missed in the weaver's cottage."

"I'll make up my work."

The heavy brows formed a scowl. "Your well-being is what is on my mind now, Harriet, not the work you have missed. Your mother was near mad when you lay ill. I do not think she could stand to lose another child." He sighed then, and looked at his hands in his lap. "Of course, there are different ways of losing one's children."

I waited, saying nothing.

"Your mother has always wanted you to leave here when your time comes, and when she gets her mind fixed on something it is like when I fix my telescope on a star. The difference being that stars move and your mother's objectives do not. Now your mother has joined forces with my son-in-law, Thomas Mann Randolph. They both tell me it is best that you go. That you want to go. Is this true, Harriet?"

If I ever get to look on the face of God, I will be not frightened. After looking into the face of Thomas Jefferson and saying yes, I want to leave this place, nothing will ever again frighten me.

He nodded his head. Then he got up and began to walk in the entranceway, his hands clasped behind him. "So, then, it is best that you go. I realize I was unfair to you at our last meeting, Harriet. I tried to impose my will upon you for my own selfish reasons. Yes, of course, I want you to stay, as I want Beverly to stay and as I wanted Tom to stay. But I must be a realist. There is nothing for you here. You are young and of a fine countenance and well bred. You must take your place in the world. And it is time, as my son-in-law has pointed out to me, to start making plans."

He paced in silence in front of me for a minute or two. All was quiet in the room except for the ticking of the seven-day clock. My heart was breaking, surely. How could it be breaking when what I was doing was right? Surely, when you do what is the right thing, your heart doesn't break, does it?

But then I looked into the face of the man who was said to be my father. And he was smiling at me. "You have made a good choice, Harriet. Difficult, but good. Mister Randolph tells me you plan to pass into the white world."

I nodded, scarcely able to speak.

"I know it pains you to cut all ties with your people. But such a move will ensure your safety. That eases my heart. But more important, it will ease the heart of your mama."

I felt a rush of joy and relief.

"I will address myself to your needs in education then. Certainly I can do that for you. Over the years I have directed the studies of several young men who asked me to do so. They placed themselves in the neighboring village and have had use of my library and counsel. You have seen them come and go. And I have taken great pains to instill a love of education in my daughters. But Mister Randolph explained all that to you, didn't he? About the books my Martha and Ellen are reading?"

"Yes, Master," I said.

"You will need to be educated for the white world, Harriet. My granddaughters, Ellen and Cornelia, studied Latin and Greek. I will not expect that from you, however. I would prefer that you read English and French literature. Although I warn you, as I have warned them, against too much fiction. Of course, you shall study history. And my Martha is more than competent to teach you French. I also hold that attention should be paid to the ornaments of life, to music and drawing and dancing. Although, Harriet," and he scowled, "I believe in the French rule that no lady should dance after marriage."

"Yes, Master." He had put so much thought into my lessons already! I could not believe it! I was so touched!

"Martha will also see to it that you are instructed in the finer domestic arts. Mister Randolph tells me you wish to marry a gentleman someday. These are all necessities for the wife of a prosperous white man, Harriet. Well, I have always said, Harriet, that the happiness of the domestic fireside is the first boon to heaven."

"I understand, Master."

"You will continue to work mornings in the weaver's

119

cottage. But each afternoon you will take your lessons with Martha. You may make use of my library, discreetly, of course. Well," and he stopped pacing and faced me, "is this all agreed upon?"

My head was swirling. Everything had moved so fast! I thanked him again.

"When you go, Harriet, I would like it to be done right. No running off into the night like Tom. Promise me you will not run off."

Tears came to my eyes. He looked so downcast. He did not want me to leave, surely, any more than I really wanted the leaving. But all he wanted from me now was my promise that I would not steal away in the night like a thief.

I promised him. He nodded gravely. "Good, good. I will keep abreast of your academic progress."

I felt dismissed, yet I lingered. For there was in the air between us some electricity. Like that made by Mister Franklin's kite. Words were left unsaid, feelings hidden. I got up, curtsied, and started to leave the room.

Harriet, he said then. He said it very low.

Yes, Master, I answered. He half turned to consider me. I waited while he, a genius with words, a maker of speeches, seemed to have difficulty picking the words he wanted to say.

"Words said can never be recalled. So it is best, oftimes, not to speak too quickly. Yet words left unsaid are worse. We wear them like weights around our hearts. So stay a moment."

I stayed.

"I have always wanted to make things as . . . pleasant

as possible around here for you and your brothers. You know that, don't you child?"

"Yes, Master."

"I have made promises to your mother. Promises I always intended to keep. She tells me you have been asking what would happen to you if I were to die. Is that true?"

Oh, I wanted to die myself then. I felt so ashamed! I grew hot and then cold, all over. He regarded me so solemnly. But I owed him the truth. "Yes, Master," I said.

"Can you tell me what prompted you to ask such a question?"

"It was said, Master, that I could be sold. If anything happened to you. If anyone else took over this place." I fell silent, terrified of the furrow that appeared in the intelligent brow.

"So that is the gossip on this place, is it?"

"I only heard it from one person, Master."

"I don't suppose you care to tell me who this one person is."

I raised my eyes to him, beseechingly. Very well, he said. I will not pursue that train of thought further. What else did this person say?

"That you are in debt, Master. Which is why I might be sold."

Blue flames crackled in his eyes. "You see me as an old man, then?"

An old man? He stood tall and straight before me. Strength radiated from him, from the span of his shoulders, the set of his head. His head was regal.

"No, Master," I said, "I see you as more command-

121

ing than the busts of George Washington and General Lafayette and Benjamin Franklin and John Paul Jones."

He laughed then. He threw his head back and laughed. "Rogue," he said. "You are as much a rogue as your brother Beverly. You choose to flatter me, then."

"No, Master, this is the truth."

He sobered. "I have enjoyed a greater share of health than falls to the lot of most men, Harriet, but I am not indestructible. So you do well to think of the future. I have debts, yes. But it is written in my will that you and your brothers shall have your freedom when your time comes. I have faith enough in Virginia law to be confident that my wishes will be carried out. Even if . . . I should die before you come of age."

Yes, Master, I said.

He nodded. He was regarding me with the most quizzical look in his eyes, as if he were trying to remember something from the past. Or as if I reminded him of something he meant to say. Only he couldn't think of it. Anyway, I know, as sure as I live and breathe, that he wanted to say more to me and was stopping himself.

"Harriet," he said. "Harriet. Where have the years gone? Leaving. Out to make your way in the world. I am glad we had this opportunity to talk. I am gratified I have time yet, to do some things for you. I would do more, child. I would petition the legislature for dispensation so you could stay in Virginia. But as I wrote to John Langdon, in 1808, when it seemed war again was imminent, 'I think one war enough for the life of one man.' "

He fell silent. Then he spoke. "You do not understand. Someday you will, child. Be off now. Come talk to me occasionally. Seek me out in the gardens or on the grounds. I will want to hear of you."

I thanked him again and curtsied. But I did not leave. I stood there, waiting. For what, I did not know, but I could not bring myself to leave yet. Something was unfinished.

He had gone back to the long windows and was gazing out, his hands clasped behind him. For a moment he seemed lost in meditation. Then, turning, he saw me standing there yet. He seemed startled.

"Was there something else, Harriet?"

"Forgive me, Master, yes."

"Well? Out with it."

"The snapdragon is blooming, Master. I saw it yesterday."

For a moment he said nothing. But the blue eyes became moist.

"Yes. Thank you, Harriet," he said. "I shall make note of it in my Farm Book. And after you go, I shall sorely miss these reminders of yours."

"When I go, Master, will everyone here say I did not exist? That there was no Harriet? Like they say about Tom?"

Tom. The mention of my brother saddened him. Did he know, I wondered, that my mama had heard from Tom that once? Did he know Tom had passed?

"Who says such things about Tom?"

"Some folk down at the quarters."

His face darkened. Then he raised his eyes to me. "We both know there was a Tom, Harriet. And I promise you I will not allow anyone here to say there was no Harriet. I promise you we will speak of you here. Always."

I bobbed another half hearted curtsy and fled the room then. I could not bear to stay a moment longer.

June 1820

In the last fortnight, I have scarcely had a minute to write in this journal. Martha Randolph keeps me as busy as a firefly on a hot June night. If I am not reading *Rousseau on Botany*, I am reading *The Vicar of Wakefield*. Or I am perfecting my penmanship. Or studying French. The only reason this June day that I have any time to write in this book is because Martha has a migraine headache. I think she inherited them from her father. The master gets them all the time. So I was sent to my room to study. But instead I must write down how it was when I first reported to Martha for lessons.

She was in the tearoom with George Wythe on her lap. The air was so still that day. Over the mountains, clouds gathered in groups, and the air felt as though you were walking through cotton. The night before had been so hot, I'd been unable to sleep, and I was tired and cross, and I found Martha just as disagreeable.

"Come out of those shadows and here into the tea-room, where I can see you," she says.

Well, there are few enough shadows in Thomas Jefferson's home to begin with. One of the greatest pleasures of his life are windows, it seems. But I presented myself for her inspection, going directly into the tearoom. Through the large windows of that room, which is octagonal in shape, I could see two more of her children playing on the lawns outside.

Close the doors, she directed, so I did so. She commenced to survey my whole person then, with those frosty blue eyes of hers. She is known never to lose her temper, never to raise her voice. I suppose there is something to be said for that, especially if you are the mother of eleven children.

"How old are you now," she asks me. So I told her. You're well past being a child, she says. Although you've been coddled and allowed to remain one far beyond your time. If my father made all you servants do a fair day's work, he might be able to make this place pay for itself. But no, he continues to cater to the lot of you.

Oh, I saw how it was going to go between us from this first encounter. But I stood there meek and humble, and listened. I know that Martha likes it when all the nigras on the place are meek and humble. And I saw no reason to provoke her at this time.

"Well," and she sighed, all breathless from her speechifying. "I do his bidding. He is my beloved father, and so I indulge his wishes. And now his wish is that I tutor you. I am not happy with the arrangement. It isn't as if I haven't enough to do around here. You don't look very happy with it yourself, do you?"

"I'll do whatever the master wishes, ma'am," I said. Something told me I should not put myself forth as happy, that if she thought all this was a burden to me, she might go easier on me.

"Well spoken. You have some measure of manners, at least."

At this point two of her children, Benjamin Franklin, who is a solemn child, and Meriwether Lewis, who is disagreeable, came into the room, begging that she allow George Wythe to come and play.

"Yes, do take him." She released the baby, kissing his damp forehead, and he toddled by and left with his brothers. Then she brushed some crumbs from her bosom, which is spotless and considerably more than sufficient.

"My father wishes me to teach you so that you may take your rightful place in the world. Do you think you know what your rightful place is?"

"I've been pondering on that, ma'am. Hoping to arrive at the answer."

"Some people never do. You intend to leave, then, when your time comes." The innocent blue eyes reminded me of a fish.

"Yes, ma'am."

"Your mother will miss you."

"Yes, ma'am."

"Children break our hearts every day. Why do we permit ourselves to love them so? Look at my son, Thomas Jefferson Randolph. He is ruining his health to come up with ways to save this place from debt,

127

and here is my father giving his nigra servants their freedom. Well," and she picked up some needlework and commenced to stitch, "I hope you know what you're about, Harriet Hemings. This whole thing is my husband's idea. I know that. I sense his hand in things. Why my father listens to him I'll never know. Thomas is having one of his brilliant fits again, I suppose. All this nonsense about introducing legislation to give Virginia's slaves their freedom. Freedom to do what, I ask? And how? Why, all the nigra servants on this place, with the exception of your mother, have to be led by the hand to eat, or they'd starve. That's how much sense they have. You think it's easy out in the world? You think all you have to do is smile and curtsy and you'll have your supper?"

I said nothing. I have known, since I was a little child, when to saying nothing in the presence of white folk. My mama taught me well.

Martha was stitching away on that man's shirt she was hemming. Then she says it to me. Without even looking up.

"You're going to pass, aren't you?"

Well, that took the breath out of me. "Ma'am?" I says.

"Don't you ma'am me. You're planning on passing. Does the master know?"

"Master knows everything that goes on around here, ma'am," I said. "That's why he's the master."

She sighed again. And the stuffings seemed to go right out of her, like a feather mattress with a big hole in it. "Well, it matters little to me. Except that I'm the one who should be told, the one you should confide

128

in. How else can I prepare you if you won't tell me? There's a vast difference in the kind of teaching I'd dispense if I knew you were passing."

But she knew, certainly! I could tell she knew I was passing. The master would have told her. "Master knows I'm passing, ma'am," I said.

"Well, Harriet Hemings, I want to hear it from your own lips. That's the *least* you could do!"

"Yes, ma'am," I said dutifully. "I'm planning on passing."

She started peering at me more like a hawk than a fish then. "Do you think being in the white world is easy, Harriet Hemings? Do you think it's like applying some of Mammy Ursula's poultices? Do you think that once you declare yourself white, all life's ills disappear?"

No, ma'am, I answered, I don't think that.

Then why are you doing it, she wants to know. So I told her. After what Mister Bankhead did to me, I told her, I knew I had to put my mind to thinking on leaving. And it isn't safe for free nigras out in the world. So I want to pass.

Well, that got her ruminating, all right. She ruminated for a full minute, and when she looked at me her eyes were soft and not at all unkind.

"I am not at all fond of my son-in-law, Charles Bankhead, Harriet," she said. "I hope this does not show a lack of charity, but I have suggested that a keeper be hired to keep him from mischief and that he be permitted to drink himself to death."

Her words startled me. But I sensed the pain behind them. I had forgotten that the same Charles Bankhead who had attacked me also beat this woman's own daughter. And I sensed, too, that this was the nearest thing to an apology I would ever get from this woman, for her son-in-law's actions.

"Thank you, ma'am," I said.

"Very well, I will teach you. History and literature and French. Drawing and music. And the domestic arts. You will learn how to do fine needlework and keep good silver in order, how to tend plants in the kitchen garden, store food for the winter, oversee soap and dye making. You will accompany me when I inspect the smokehouse, the icehouse, the fowls. You will learn to play the pianoforte and appear fresh in the morning after being up all night with a sick child. And you will be instructed in dancing when the dance master comes, twice a month, to teach my children."

I said thank you.

"You will practice penmanship so you can correspond with the wife of a statesman, if necessary. But for now, you will pour me another cup of tea."

My hands trembled as I performed the task. "Where did you learn to pour so well," she asked. I said Mama had taught me.

"I have been the mistress of Monticello since 1809," she said.

I said, yes, ma'am.

"Your mama knows a great deal, but you will do things as I instruct. Not as you learned them from your mama."

"Yes, ma'am."

"As the mistress of Monticello, I will teach you all you need to know. When I get finished with you, you

130

will know how to behave in the President's house if necessary. But I will not tolerate laziness or bad manners. I have heard you sass your mama. You will not sass me."

I agreed to that, too.

"I am not fond of you, Harriet Hemings. I will not pretend that I am. There are altogether too many Hemings on this place to suit me. But I will carry out my father's wishes and make a lady of you. My father is very dear to me. And as his only surviving child there is little I would not do to make him happy."

Ah, I thought, so there it was. There was what was between us, laid bare, finally, like some old chicken bones that wouldn't be buried. So this is the way it is going to be between us, I thought. There will be no pleasing her. Not until I am gone away from here. My very presence is a burr in her shoe.

Ah, well, I thought, I will live through this. And then there will be one less Hemings around to remind her of things she would prefer not to contemplate, even though those things be as vaporous as the clouds over the Blue Ridge. Which are sometimes as wondrous-looking as pink cotton. And other times so black and threatening that they make one fear for one's soul.

Early July 1820

I was kept so busy over the next month, what with my chores in the weaver's cottage and my lessons, that I had little time to see anyone. Then yesterday afternoon, Martha declared a day off and sent me outside for some fresh air. She said I looked tired. To tell the truth, I think she was tired. But I can't fault her. She has done her duty by me and acted tolerable, if not amiable. It is more than I could expect.

It is early July now. Everyone is in the fields, harvesting the wheat. The wheat harvest began on the twenty-ninth of June this year, and every available body on the place, except those who work in the carpentry and nailery, is working in the fields.

In the carpentry and nailery shops, they must repair broken tools, so the harvest can go on uninterrupted. The master said the wheat must be harvested in eleven days. This is because around the twelfth of July, he wants to start cutting the rye.

My brother Madison has been working in the carpenter's shop for the past year under John Hemings. Eston still does light duties around the house. But when I found out I was free this afternoon, I found Eston, and we ran to the carpenter's shop to beg John Hemings to release Madison for a while. We wanted to pick the last of the raspberries growing around the terraces at the southwest end of the vegetable garden.

John Hemings, being the youngest son of my grandmother Elizabeth Hemings, could not refuse us. So he let Mad go.

We filled our cups with the raspberries and settled under the nearest tree to enjoy them. No sooner had we sat down than my brothers commenced to ask me questions.

"You like your new lessons with Martha?" Mad wanted to know.

I noticed how like Beverly he is starting to look. His shoulders are getting bigger, and he is gaining in stature every day. I told him I liked my lessons well enough, but Martha acted as if she were always sucking on lemons.

They laughed at that. Then Mad said she had no reason to be such a sourpuss. "Master got it fixed so she's the mistress 'round here, not Mama. She even gives out the clothes to Mama."

"She does that to remind Mama who she is," I told them. "It's a mortification Mama has to bear."

"She doesn't like me," Madison said. "Because the

master takes so much time to see I play my fiddle real proper like."

Madison is fast becoming a first-rate fiddle player. He is a quiet young man, I mark here. He has sandy hair and gray eyes, and is greatly attached to Mama. And Eston is following in his footsteps as far as music is concerned.

Then Madison gave me a look, sly as a fox. "You getting ready to stroll, Harriet?" he asks me.

My heart went out then to my two younger brothers. For I saw them waiting for my answer. You both know I'm leaving when my time comes, I told them. I'm not strolling.

Eston kept his eyes to the ground. Madison just nodded. I told them we all have to go when our time comes.

"Beverly isn't going," Eston said.

Well, I said, he should be. "He isn't doing himself any good around here."

"Bev's getting bad," Eston said. "He's got no happiness in him anymore."

"He's got things to ponder," Madison said.

What kind of things, I asked. But Mad just shook his head. "Come on, Mad," I urged. "No secrets. We promised each other we'd share."

So he told me then. "Bev says you're gonna pass."

I just held my breath. They were staring at me. So then, Bev had found out somehow. Oh, how my heart ached for him. And I had not even been given the opportunity to tell him myself! Oh, I felt a spasm in my heart. How could I justify myself to him?

"Are you?" Madison was asking.

Well, there was nothing for it but to say yes. "I have to," I said. "As I am given to understand that in the outside world I wouldn't be safe as a free nigra."

"What's the sense in being free, then?" Eston asked.

"Free is better," I told them. "Free is always better. But free white is better than free nigra. You always have to carry papers as a free nigra. And sometimes, even with those papers, they come after you. And sometimes those papers don't help you at all."

"When I grow up," Eston said, "I'm gonna be a great musician. Won't matter if I'm nigra. Important white people in Richmond and Charlottesville will invite me to their homes to play. And they'll pay me."

"If you take your freedom and stay nigra, you have to leave Virginia," I told him. "It's the law."

"Then I'll go west," Eston said. "Or north."

But Madison was eyeing me like a fox eyeing a chicken. "That's a big step, Harriet. Passing."

I told him I knew.

He shook his head and plucked the grass around his legs. "I don't know why it has to be this way. We all want to grow up, but what it means is we have to leave and never see each other again. Why should this be?"

It's the way of things, I told them. It's because of whose children we are.

"You think we're his children, Harriet?" Eston said.

There it was again. And, oh, their eyes were fastened on me as if I knew the truth. How I wished I could give them a proper answer.

135

"I don't know," I said. "Bev thinks it is so. But I have no proof."

"Mama?" Eston asked hopefully.

I shook my head. "Mama won't say."

"Not fair not knowing," Eston said.

"He loves us," I told them. "He does his best by us. It's the same as if we were."

"Wish he'd tell us," Madison said.

He can't, I told them. Oh, I felt so old suddenly. Or did they just seem so young and innocent. I could never tell them what brought me to my decision to leave. Nor did I want them to know about this business of being sold if the master died. "He can't show it more," I told them. "It would make trouble. For him and for Mama and for us."

"Beverly is angry with him," Madison said.

Well, Beverly has some growing up to do, I suggested. And it's better he doesn't leave yet, because he probably isn't ready.

Madison got to his feet. He tied his pewter cup around his waist with a piece of rawhide. "I have to get back. Mister Bacon's always jawing about John giving me privileges."

Our nice afternoon was over. I got up, too, and so did Eston. More than the afternoon was over, I was feeling. My childhood with my brothers was finished. We were growing apart. I could feel it. I reached out to put a hand on each of them. I drew them to me until our heads touched.

"Listen," I said. "Because of who we are, no matter where we go, we'll always be together in our hearts. We have to take our chances and leave when our time

136

comes. But what we are in spirit they can't take from us."

They agreed with me, but I knew in my bones they were saying it just to make me happy. And I became more desolate than ever. Madison pulled away first. "I think I'll stay past my time. To be with Mama. Someone has to stay with Mama. He won't live forever, you know."

Over Eston's head, Madison met my eyes. So he knows, too, I thought. About the master being old and in debt. But he wouldn't utter that before Eston.

"Oh, Mad!" I threw my arms around him. He hugged me tight.

"Don't you worry about anything, Harriet," he said. "You just set your mind on your lessons so you're ready when your time comes. We'll be fine. I'll take care of Mama."

I felt a sense of peace come over me. Madison was older than his fifteen years proclaimed. I sensed that now. He knew things beyond his years. He just didn't go jawing about them like Beverly or Thruston. But in the gold flecks in his solemn brown eyes I had seen a maturity and courage I'd never noticed before.

"Gotta get back," he said, squeezing me. "Why don't you two enjoy the rest of the afternoon?"

He moved away, up the terraced slope. I turned to Eston. "Let's get your fiddle, and you can play for me," I said.

We walked back toward the house. "You know what I wish?" Eston said. "I wish he didn't treat us so nice. Makes us think we're his children. It's like being birds and not being able to fly. Like that baby bird Cromwell the cat caught in the spring. Hurt its wing. And it couldn't fly. You remember how it just hopped across the lawn, Harriet?"

Well, I was struck dumb hearing that. And I'd thought Eston still a baby. Now I find that he, too, has wisdom beyond his years. And then I thought — how can any of us be babies? Nigra children never are. We, all of us, are more nigra than white.

The temperature has climbed to ninety-eight degrees as I write this. It was so hot in the weaver's cottage today, even with all the windows open, that I thought I would perish. I was wearing my lightest chemise, and I sat at the loom with my skirts hiked up around my knees in a most unladylike fashion. The scant breeze fanned my legs. The other girls, Celia, who is fourteen, and Anne who is fifteen, did the same thing.

It is two days since my conversation with my brothers. I thought about it all morning as I worked. At noon the steady thumping of the looms stopped, and we were released to have our meal, which was ready for us in the cool underground kitchen.

But Celia and Anne ran laughing out of the cottage. I heard them whispering and giggling about Jupiter, who is sixteen and working in the fields as a binder.

As I walked down Mulberry Row, I could hear the shouts and laughter of the cradlers, binders, stackers, and gatherers as the harvest was being reaped. It is now the eighth of July.

I walked slowly. Ahead of me Anne and Celia ran barefoot toward the fields. I could tell where the workers were by the circle of crows in the sky where they were cutting. At noon everything will come to a stop. And my mama and the house help will portion out food in the fields. There will be laughter and joking as the servants gather to eat. Anne and Celia will be there, I thought, with the rest of the day off. They will be near Jupiter. And he'll display his sixteen-year-old muscled arms to them. How stupid!

Where would it all lead? Where would it get them? One of them will marry Jupiter and have baby after baby down in the slave cabins.

But then it came to me that there wasn't anything else for Celia and Anne. And I told myself how fortunate I was. And then I asked myself why, if I'm so fortunate, am I so miserable?

Because it's been a month now since I spoke to Mister Randolph that day under the tree and made plans to leave. But the only leaving done around here was by him. And he's not come by since, not even late at night, soaked to the skin after fording a river on his horse.

Why doesn't he come? Why don't I hear something from him? Has he forgotten? Was he having, as his wife said, one of his brilliant fits? Is it over now? What's to become of me? What's all this studying for? Oh, I was tired. I had a headache and my back hurt from sitting at the loom and I would have given anything to be as simpleminded as Anne and Celia, laughing with Jupiter under the crystal-blue sky and drinking cold cider and eating ham and cold biscuits.

And then, just up ahead, I saw Beverly step out of the carpentry. I ran to catch up to him, but he kept right on walking. I called his name. Then I caught up with him and fell into step and tugged his sleeve. "Uppity," I said to him.

"Who says?"

"I say."

"You're one to talk. Where you been? Too good for us common folk anymore?"

"Bev, I have duties."

"Duties. Ha! You think everybody on this place doesn't know what you're up to?"

"Oh, I suspect they do, Bev. There isn't much that goes on around here that everybody doesn't know about."

He stopped then to scowl at me. His eyes were hard as flints. He's going to get into trouble someday, I thought, if he doesn't stop being so ornery. Oh, Lordy, this is my brother. What happened to him? What's turned him from a laughing boy into a bitter, suspicious man?

But I knew that, didn't I?

"You know what you're up to, all right," he said. "You're gonna pass, aren't you, Harriet?"

Well, I said nothing. What could I say?

"Ain't that so, sister of mine?"

"Yes, Bev," I said. No sense trying to fool him. "Tom did. That's what Mama told me." I didn't know if she'd told him the same thing about Tom that she'd told me, but he seemed to know. He spat in the dirt.

"Tom. He broke Mama's heart when he left. You think that hasn't broken her heart?"

"You're breaking her heart just as much in another way," I said. "Staying here. Mouthing off to Eston

140

and Madison the way you've been lately. Mama wants you to leave, Bev. Her heart will break if you *stay*. There's different ways of breaking a body's heart, Bev."

"That the kind of stuff Martha Randolph teaching you?"

"She doesn't have to teach me. I just know it myself."

He looked at the ground then, scuffed it with his toe.

"You're so full of anger, Bev. You stay that way and soon you'll shrivel up and blow away like that balloon you made."

"I don't wanna talk about it," he said.

"You should, Bev. Whatever's inside you is festering. It will give you a mortification of the spirit."

"What's festering inside me is that my only sister is passing into the white world and turning her back on her people."

There it was. Out now. Better it was out. He felt betrayed.

"I'm passing, yes, Bev. I decided to. But not to turn my back on my people. I can never do that."

"You have a different meaning for what you're doing then, sister?"

"I'm being sensible, Bev. The world out there isn't safe for a free nigra. And I'm light enough to pass."

I looked at him, but his eyes were stone hard. "Keep talking," he said.

So that wasn't enough for him. No, it wouldn't be. Knowing Bev I realized that he'd feel that if I was going to take my freedom I should take it as a nigra.

That kind of thinking was part of his misery right now. "We're part white anyways, Bev. Don't forget that. I think the master raised us so we could make it in the white world if we wanted to. Else, why did he educate us?"

"Because Mama got the promise of freedom for us."

"That's right, Bev. So he knew all along we'd be going. We're taking what's rightfully ours."

"What's rightfully ours could be ours if we stayed right here," he said. "What is ours, by rights, you ever ask yourself, Harriet?"

"There's days I don't know, Bev. You think it doesn't bother me? There's days I know I'm nigra, and what's mine is in those cabins down there. Days when I know it so much that I hate myself for wanting to leave, let alone pass! Then, other times I know I'm different. There's times I *want* more, Bev. Times I know I *deserve* more! Because of who I am. And then I feel so guilty about it."

"And who are you, sister?" he asked.

"You always said we were his children, Bev. And if it's true, then that's the part of me that wants more. And I can't help the wanting. Oh, Bev, don't be angry with me. I'm so confused."

He said nothing for a moment, and I was so frightened. But there was plenty going on behind those eyes of his.

"So you believe me when I tell you we're his children, then," he said.

"I don't know what I believe, Bev. I'd rather believe it than not. It comforts me. Because then on the days

142

when I desire more than all the other nigra servants around here, I don't feel so guilty about it."

"How do you know they don't want the same things as you?" he asked.

"I see Celia and Anne," I said. "And I know all they care about is getting Jupiter's attention."

"They have no chance for anything else. And they know it," he said.

He was right! Oh, he was so right! But I responded quickly. "So then, if I have the chance, shouldn't I take it, Bev?"

Again he did not answer.

"Thruston said that if the master dies before I come of age, I could be sold. You're already of age. You can take your freedom anytime. You can take it tomorrow if the master dies. But I have two more years. You want me to be sold, Bev?"

He looked past me, toward the fields. I saw his eyes searching the hard blue sky. He sighed and shook his head slowly. "'Course I don't want you to be sold, Harriet," he said softly.

"And what about what Charles Bankhead did to me? You think I want that to happen again, Bev?"

"No." He shook his head sadly. "I'm sorry about that, Harriet. Mama told me what happened. And how Thruston and Mister Randolph and Burwell came to your aid. If I'd been there I'd have run Bankhead through with a knife."

"Better you weren't there, then, Bev. We don't need that kind of trouble around here. He'll get his come-uppance, don't worry. He hasn't a friend around here anymore. Not even Martha Randolph. But you see now, why I have to think on my future. And why Mister Randolph is helping me. You're a man and you've got your freedom any time you want it. I'm a woman, Bev, and I have to wait two more years for mine. I'm in more danger than you."

He nodded, listening, but I could tell something was still worrying away at him. "That why you're planning on marrying a high-falutin' white man?"

I said nothing then. How could I? It came to me that I'd been foolish to try to keep that part of my plan from Beverly. How had he found out about that? Had Mama told him? No, I decided, Mama knew when to keep her own good counsel. But if not Mama, then who?

Oh, what did it matter? There were no secrets on this place, and I was stupid to try to keep any. Everything that happened inside the big house on the hill of an evening was talk, next morning, in the cabins on Mulberry Row. I raised my eyes to see him glaring at me, waiting for an explanation.

"Things have moved so fast, Bev," I said.

"I'd say they had, sister."

"Mister Randolph swore me to secrecy. Not even the master knows about this man who Mister Randolph says is interested in making my acquaintance. But after what Charles Bankhead did to me, Bev, Mister Randolph thought it would protect me over these next two years, if everyone knew I was betrothed."

"To a white man," he breathed.

"Bev, I'm *passing* as white!"

"Exactly," he said. "Taking your freedom is one

thing, but passing is what we're talking about, Harriet."

Oh, I was so weary of this! He was so stubborn! And then I had another thought. "You remember Mama's brother, James?"

"No. He died in 1801. Year you were birthed. So you don't recollect him, either."

"What I mean, Bev, is you remember hearing how he killed himself?"

"I heard tell of it."

"Well, I've pondered on that, too. The master freed him. Just gave him his papers and let him go. He went as a nigra. Look what happened."

"He was crazy," Bev said.

"He was trained as a French chef by the master in Paris. He and Mama were educated in Paris together. He had a better means of making a living than anybody. And he killed himself. Now, why, do you suppose?"

"I haven't considered it," he said. "But not all free nigras kill themselves."

"Well, I have considered it. I've pondered on all sides of this problem, Bev. I gnawed it down like a bone. And when I got all done, one thing I've figured for sure. And that is that it must be a terrible thing being a free nigra out there. Free, but only able to do what white folks say you can do. But it must be worse being a free nigra with the education of a white person. Like James had. And like we have. Why else would James have killed himself?"

"I don't know, Harriet," he said softly. "But you've beaten me down with arguments. I can see that. I've

145

got no worries about you making it out there in the white world. You have one quick mind, woman. Like a fox."

I smiled hesitantly at him, though tears sprang into my eyes. Had he forgiven me for what I was about to do then?

"I wish you the best, Harriet," he said quietly.

"You do, Bev?"

"Sure I do. I only wish I could think like you. But I can't."

"I'll pray for you, Bev," I said.

He laughed. "You do that, little sister. You do that."

Oh, my heart breaks every time I think about Beverly. There is a sickness inside me when I see him, scowling all the time and so disagreeable, a sickness that sits like a rock in my innards. It travels through my blood and I can't be rid of it. It hangs over me like one of Mammy's curses. And when I'm languishing about and enjoying my studies, as I often do, or taking some small pleasure in some new task, I stop and the sickness is there in my innards.

Like a poison. It kills all my happiness. It impoverishes my spirit. Doesn't anyone else on this place see what is happening to Beverly? Am I the only one?

Oh, sometimes I think I have a disorder of the mind!

October 1820

Oh, I am so happy! I had to take time today to record it in my book. After months of wondering and being distressed because I have not heard from Mister Randolph, I have received a letter from him. Master gave it to me today.

I broke the seal and rushed off to read it alone. I do believe it is the first letter I have ever received from anyone in my life.

So I felt very important reading it. He inquired about my studies and said he heard my progress was favorable. He suggested I take my quill pen in hand and write to him so he might judge for himself my ability to correspond.

Then he suggested I show the letter to Martha so she could give me his proper address. I did so, and Martha made me sit down immediately to reply. She took it all as praise for her efforts at teaching me, of course. I write here that it is to my credit that I did not detract from Martha's satisfaction.

Within a fortnight of sending the reply off, another letter from Mister Randolph arrived for me.

I did not show this one to Martha. In the first paragraph he admonished me to show this correspondence to no one.

Perhaps next summer, he wrote, a visitor will arrive at Monticello. He is an acquaintance of Mister Jefferson's.

He wrote that he could tell me no more now, but that he hoped I would be pleased with the gentleman. And that, when he made future visits to Monticello, between now and then, it would be best if we were not seen conspiring but went about our normal paths. Then he said I would be best advised to destroy the letter. So I did.

June 1821

It is summer again. I have been extremely remiss because I have not written in this journal since last autumn. But my studies took all my time. Every night I fell into bed in exhaustion.

The master has told me he is pleased with my progress. And Mister Randolph, to whom I have faithfully written several letters and who has visited here often, has said the same thing. Of course, in accordance with Mister Randolph's wishes, when he visits I behave with the utmost decorum. And do not act as if we are conspiring about anything. Yet most of the nigra servants seem to know something is amiss with me, but are not sure what.

Mama says I walk slower these days. And I no longer sit idle but am always busy with some fine needlework like a well-bred lady.

"When I was fifteen," Martha told me, "my father wrote me a letter saying that the needle is a valuable resource. In country life in America, he explained, there are moments when a woman can have recourse to nothing but her needle. When one has company, for instance, it is ill-mannered to read and, of course, card playing is not for 'genteel people,' he explained. I now give you the benefit of my father's beliefs, Harriet."

My younger brothers complain that I no longer argue or tumble about with them. Yet they seem gratified that I listen to them recite their lessons and play their music.

Thruston has told me, mockingly, that he sees changes in me. He says I lower my eyes most decorously when I speak to a man. He laughs at me when I rail out at him in French. But I know he is proud of me. I can see it in his eyes. For when I speak with Thruston, I do not lower my eyes decorously. I look right at him.

Late June 1821

Oh, it is so hot! The heat of this June seems to lay in waves of whiteness over this whole place. The drone

149

of insects is like a form of madness, always there in the mind. It is too hot to eat, to work, to do anything. My limbs feel as if they are made of molasses. And this place is full of company, as always, in the summer. All Martha's children seem to be about in one form or another. The houseguests overrun us this summer. People have to be put up on makeshift mattresses in the upstairs hallways, there are so many guests.

For the most part, I stay out of the house. I prefer the weaver's cottage to the tasks of carrying trays of cold lemonade to the visiting ladies as they languish in the parlor or outside under the trees.

Of course, Martha Randolph always summons me to help when I am not in the weaver's cottage. "I might as well have benefit of something of what I've taught you," she says. "You'll be gone soon enough. Small payment for all my efforts if I ask you to play the pianoforte after supper for our guests. Can't you see how tired your mama is? Come now, take this tray of tea cakes to the ladies on the east portico."

And so I would. For Mama does look so weary. She constantly has to oversee the servants in the round of food preparation, in the airing of the bedding, and the flow of clean and laundered clothing.

And in the midst of all this they have already started to cut the wheat. So the master is out in the fields on his horse under the hard blue sky all day and entertaining his guests in the evening.

I have come back to write in this journal because something of great importance has happened in my life. The gentleman Mister Randolph had in mind for me has come to Monticello.

Oh, I have met him! I have met him! I can barely write these words, I am trembling so from head to toe.

I get fever and shakes when I think of the crinkles around his eyes, and the way his teeth show so generously when he laughs. I feel my very bones turn to mush under his steadfast gaze. Oh, to think I never felt I would allow a man to get me in such a state!

But let me write here how I came to know he was at Monticello.

I was sauntering, yesterday, on the roundabout walk on the west lawn. I had just returned from delivering a tray of lemonade and tea cakes to some visiting ladies who have nothing else to do all day but take their ease and gossip and conspire to stay cool.

As I walked along, I looked up, and there was Mister Randolph coming toward me. He was alone.

"Harriet, I have been looking for you," he said.

I curtsied and he smiled.

"My wife is most pleased with your progress, and, as you know, Harriet, Martha is not easily pleased."

He stood there in God's good sunlight, this dear man, clasping and unclasping his hands like a schoolboy before me. He seemed most agitated. He mopped his brow with his handkerchief.

"I understand you are getting most proficient in the domestic arts," he said.

"Yes, Mister Randolph, thank you."

"Then you wouldn't be put off if you were asked to serve a certain gentleman tea in the tearoom? The way you were that morning so long ago now, when your mama asked you to serve my breakfast?"

I blushed. There was a special note of breathlessness in his voice. And when I looked up at him, he was smiling in a most kindly way. I put my hand to my throat. And I felt my head spin beneath the spiraling blue sky. What was he telling me? Could it be possible?

It could and it was. The man he had chosen for me was, this minute, at Monticello! One of the many guests who swarmed about the lawns like a plague of locusts.

"No, sir," I said with much dignity. "I wouldn't be put off by that."

"Good, good. Then go to the kitchen. Your mama knows and will instruct you."

"But it isn't teatime, sir," I said.

"It is time, Harriet Hemings," he said. "Do not question the hour. Only now will you be able to spend some time with him in the tearoom. The house is deserted."

I do not recall the next half hour at all. I do recollect that in the underground kitchen, Mama had clean clothes for me and bade me wash. The soap she gave me was scented, and the fragrance lingered on my arms and face and shoulders.

Then I slipped into a new chemise of the softest lawn, a striped petticoat, and a snow-white apron. "All these clothes are new, Mama," I said wonderingly.

Nothing we wore was new. Only sometimes we got rough homespun.

"Hush," she said.

But I realized these were from the parcel of clothing

she had made for me. Tears came to my eyes.

Quickly she combed my hair and rebraided it so that a few wisps of reddish curls framed my face, softening my appearance. Then she placed a dainty white starched mobcap on my head and announced that I was ready.

She would send tea up on the dumbwaiter. All this time she never uttered a word about who was in the tearoom. I begged her for some scrap of information.

She kissed me. "I don't want to set your mind, one way or another. Just go now."

I was in a state of agitated despair. "What shall I do to please him, Mama?"

"Just be Harriet Hemings."

So I went.

Oh, I thought, rushing through the underground corridor, if only I had time to go to Mammy Ursula for some good voodoo. The house was so quiet, as if everyone had been spirited out of sight. I had a feeling of moving through time itself. I saw myself as a small, scurrying animal rushing into my future. But I was not afraid.

He was at the table in the tearoom, reading a newspaper. The double doors of the tearoom obscured his features, but I could make out the form of a well-dressed man with good shoulders and a full head of hair the color of chestnuts.

I fetched the tea service from the dumbwaiter, and before I reached the doors of the tearoom, he got to his feet and opened them. Then he took the tea service from me and set it on the table, leaving me there to fuss with my hands like I was dim-witted.

I was not accustomed to such solicitude. I curtsied. Then I stood there like Lot's wife in the Bible. Struck dumb and blind. I felt his gaze upon me.

"Harriet," he said.

Then he took my hand and kissed it.

Lordy save me, I prayed. I am not much with prayers. I haven't decided yet whether I believe more in the Christian God or in Mammy Ursula's witches and demons. I felt like beeswax on a hot day, like I was melting right into the floor. Then I looked into his face.

Oh, it is a good face. There is no secret sin written there. The crinkles around the eyes are from laughter, not from conspiring and greed. The nose is very strong and aristocratic. A lock of curly hair falls over his forehead. His skin is ruddy, as if he enjoys many outdoor activities. He is just about as tall as the master. I take him to be no older than twenty-seven.

"Harriet," he said again. "Sit, do, please. I have wanted, for so long, to meet you."

I settled down inside myself then. The way he said my name calmed me. I could be calm around this man, I told myself. I could be comfortable.

"Do sit," he said again.

"I must serve the tea, sir," I said.

"Oh, yes, the tea. Very well. Pour two cups."

"Sir," I hesitated, "I daren't."

"Oh?" And one eyebrow went up. "And why daren't you?"

"If anyone saw me sitting at this table with you, I'd be punished."

"I will not allow it, Harriet."

Still I stood there, undecided, wanting to please him and remembering years of my training in this house.

"I've distressed you," he said.

"Yes, sir, you have."

He nodded. "My roots are Northern, Harriet. I was educated at Harvard. Although I've lived in the South these last eight years, its ways come hard to me. I apologize for distressing you. But there is no one about. You would do me a great honor to sit and have tea with me."

I looked into his eyes again. And I mark here that what I saw there was a light of kindness as I have never seen in any man's eyes. Not even the master's. So I made my decision.

I poured two cups of tea. Mama had sent up two cups on the tray, so this must be what she intended. Then I sat down.

He watched my every movement with studied interest. I picked up the plate of biscuits and jam and fresh sweet butter and set it forth before him. He smiled and stirred sugar into his cup.

"I understand you leave Monticello within a year," he said softly.

Yes, sir, I said.

"Mister Randolph, who is a friend of mine, tells me you wish to pass into the white world and marry."

Oh! Oh! I felt faint. I cast my gaze at him beseechingly. He smiled kindly.

"I am sorry again if I've distressed you. I am an outspoken man, Harriet. There isn't time for the usual amenities. We have only this one meeting and much to discuss. I will be as discreet as possible. May I continue?"

I whispered yes.

"I have been to Monticello before, as you know. As an architect and a member of the citizenry, I admire Mister Jefferson and have benefited from his counsel. He has allowed me to use his library. But on my visits here, over the years, something has always distressed me."

I raised my eyes to meet his. The intensity of his gaze burned right into me.

"What has distressed me is that the man who defined the noble principle of freedom for us all should keep slaves."

I said nothing. My face burned.

"Drink your tea, Harriet," he admonished. "I do not expect a response from you. I only beg that you listen."

I sipped my tea.

"The question of slavery has always haunted me. As it should haunt every American who has a conscience. But, like so many others who abhor slavery, I found myself even more horrified whenever I came across slaves like yourself and your brothers, who look and act as whites do. Don't get me wrong, Harriet, I'm not saying that because your skin is almost white you should be free while others around here remain slaves. I am saying that when one comes face to face with a person who is almost white and that person is a slave, it underscores the awfulness of the practice we have allowed to come to pass in this country."

I nodded, fully entranced by what he was saying.

"I know many people who thought they approved of slavery, Harriet, until they met, on some plantation in their travels, a slave as light-skinned as yourself. And that pushed them off the fence as far as deciding what side they came down on concerning the problem. Because, what it tells us, Harriet, is that we have made a slave of the African, but we have used his women for our own pleasures. Do you understand?"

"Yes," I said clearly.

"And so it affected me whenever I came here and saw you and your brothers. It bothered me even more when I heard the whispers that you might, indeed, be the children of the great Thomas Jefferson himself. And then, when Mister Randolph told me that your freedom was assured when you all became twenty-one, I thought, But what will happen to the children of this great man? Will they just be allowed to disappear?"

I was trembling. What he was saying had me under a spell.

"When we first came face to face, Harriet, you were running and playing out on the lawns. It was about five years ago. You looked up into my face and for a moment, I saw, in you, the heartbreak of the whole slave system."

He set his tea cup down. "You've always haunted me, Harriet. Then Mister Randolph told me how your brother Tom ran off, never to return. I could not bear that happening to you. I could not bear thinking you might have to make your way out in that world alone. I know it is only a whisper that you may be his children. But the mere possibility of it makes me want to cry out to heaven for justice. Would you pour me more tea?"

I did. Then he spoke again.

"I have spoken to your mother, whom I consider to be a fine woman. I feel as if I have watched you grow up. And then, within the last year, Mister Randolph mentioned to me that you were going to take your freedom. He knew I would be interested in helping to see that you got safe passage."

I felt tears in my eyes.

"Drink your tea, Harriet. You would gratify me if you did."

I wanted to gratify him. Oh, yes, I did. So I sipped my tea, holding onto my cup for dear life. For I feared I would be pulled into the depths of his brown eyes. In them was an invitation for me not to be afraid. He sat back in his chair, crossing one leg over the other, and gazed out the windows.

"They're harvesting the rye today," he said. "I helped yesterday. I intended to help today. But I wanted to have this meeting with you. I leave tomorrow and I must pack."

Leave? My heart lurched. But he smiled serenely. "I am not one of those people who would take advantage of Mister Jefferson's hospitality. Mister Randolph tells me some people come for a fortnight and stay the summer. It's a wondrous thing the man is still able to feed his own family, with such a drain on his resources. And at his age, he is on his horse in the fields. One must admire him."

"The master rides every day," I said.

"Do you always call him master, then?"

"Yes, sir."

"And why?"

"Because that's what he is."

He said nothing. "He takes care of us," I said. "He gives us everything."

"You work for what you get, do you not?"

I smiled. "Others do. I don't work that hard. Martha Randolph says the master spoils the lot of us."

He smiled. "Ah, the ambiguity of all this. How confused Thomas Jefferson must be about slavery. You are secure and loved here, then. And yet you choose to leave. Why?"

"Because I want to be free. I don't want to be a slave." Surely I could not confide more in this man. Not even for all his kindness. Someday, perhaps, but not now, I could tell him of what had happened with Charles Bankhead, of my fears of the master dying and being sold.

"In the world you will go into, no one has a master, Harriet. You will work for your own keep. Unless you have a husband. And then he will provide for you."

I told him that was most agreeable to me.

"Won't you miss all this if you go?" And he waved his hand, including in one gesture the whole of Monticello.

Yes, I told him. But if I stay I will come to hate it.

He nodded. "You have learned that already."

And he studied me more closely then. "You have courage, Harriet. Thomas told me you are spirited. It will serve you well. May I now be even more honest?"

I held my breath. What would this man say next? But I nodded yes.

"Thomas approached me, knowing of my interest in you. I will not lead you to think that I have not been interested in other women over the years, or that, having seen you five years ago I was totally smitten and could think of no one else. That is not true. You were a child then. What I felt for you and your brothers and your situation then was concern. And outrage. I knew I could do nothing about it. I never thought of doing anything. Come, Harriet, don't look so frightened. I'm not going to say anything to compromise you."

I blushed and sipped my tea. Cold now, but I sipped for dear life.

"Every time I saw you, of course, your . . . condition and situation came fresh in the forefront of my mind. I always left here disturbed. The last two times I visited here, I must confess, I was completely taken with you and the way you have become such a charming young lady."

Tea. More tea, I thought. But I could not bring myself to break the spell and reach for the pot.

"Of course, I never thought of you in any way that . . ." He hesitated now, shook his head, and smiled in a most amiable manner. "I'm doing this badly. I never expected to be able to help you. Then, when Thomas asked if I could, I said yes immediately.

"Well," he went on, "his plan is . . ." Again he hesitated.

"He's looking for a husband for me," I said.

Lordy, I don't know what made me come out with it like that. But I couldn't bear to see the poor man suffer.

160

A smile suffused his face. "Yes. This is devilishly awkward, Harriet. He told me you not only needed safe passage into the white world, you needed to be betrothed or they might marry you off here. And then you will be stuck here as a slave. So I told him I would meet with you. And if it was agreeable to you we'd say, within a proper time, that your betrothal would be arranged in the outside world. Mister Jefferson would have to approve, of course. But it would be kept a secret, so your passage into the white world would go smoothly."

He stopped talking and looked at me. "But hear me out, now. I'll not have you go from one master to another. You will have all you can do to start afresh in a new world. I would be honored if you would allow me to help you make your way in it, Harriet Hemings. But I'll force you into no decision concerning me. I have the advantage of having known you for some time now. You do not know me. I would have you taste freedom first. With no conditions attached to it. I do not wish to be a new master. I wish to be your friend."

"Oh, sir!" I was so touched by his gentle words, spoken so simply, and accompanied by that warm smile and those sun-flecked brown eyes, that I covered my face with my hands.

He started to get up then. "I've distressed you again."

"No, no. It's just that you are so kind. I never expected . . ."

He sat back down. "And I never expected the good fortune of being asked to help you attain your freedom.

I look forward to this, Harriet, more than anything. It means much to me. Now, we have other considerations to discuss, and time grows short. I live in Washington City. Are you willing to come there when you leave here?"

"Oh, yes, sir. I would love to see Washington City!"

"What do you plan to do to support yourself?"

But I had not thought on that. I sobered. He would be disappointed in me now. He would consider me nothing but a silly girl. A slave girl. And not worthy of his attention, for I could not even think for myself.

I just stared at him. "I can cook," I said, "and sew. And — "

"No, Harriet, no." He pushed his chair from the table and got to his feet. "No, that won't do. At all."

That Same Day

I am obliged to mark the truth here, which is that for the moment, my heart fell inside me as I watched him stand up to his full height. He is taller than the master, I am sure. He walked to the tearoom windows and gazed out. A dreadful silence fell in the room. Then he spoke without turning to look at me.

"What about teaching, Harriet? You are well educated."

I just stared at him in wonderment.

"My sister, who is married, is very involved with the Washington Orphan Asylum. It was started in 1815 to clothe, feed, and educate female orphans. They have a house on northwest Tenth Street, near Pennsylvania Avenue."

I felt so lost. The richness of his voice played across my mind.

With a faint smile playing about his lips, he turned around now to look at me. "Well, Harriet, is what I propose agreeable to you?"

My hand went to my throat. "Sir, I have never been down the mountain except to go to a neighboring plantation and help out when there was a barbecue or a frolic. You speak of Washington City. To me it is another world."

"I will help you make an entrance into that world, Harriet. Don't be frightened by it. You underestimate yourself. You were raised and tutored here at Monticello, in the home of one of the greatest men in America. Surely it counts for something."

"Do you honestly think I could teach?" I asked.

"Why not?" he answered. "You speak French. You are well versed in sums and geography. You know music, dancing, and needlework. My sister would be gratified to have you. And you would be paid for your work. You'll need a place to live, also, until . . ." He hesitated. ". . . until your future is established."

And now he blushed and gazed at his boots.

"You can live with my sister and her husband if you wish."

I thanked him and told him I would like that very much.

"You may stay at my sister's as long as you wish. Earn your own wages for a while. Go your way with no obligation to me. I would hope to be able to call upon you, of course, and offer my counsel and perhaps show you the city. If, when we become friends, you decide to go your own way, you may. You must make this decision for yourself, Harriet. I insist upon it."

He smiled sadly. "We must come to know each other away from this place to realize if we are suited for each other, Harriet."

I raised my eyes to him beseechingly. "I've already decided that we are well suited," I said. Oh, I don't know what made me so bold! But I said it plain, then clamped my mouth shut.

"No." He shook his head. "No. I cannot take advantage of your innocence. You need time. As a white woman you must learn that you have no master."

I was confused.

"What is it?" he asked.

"I've already been bold, sir. I don't want to be impertinent."

"Be impertinent, Harriet. Do. Please."

Hesitantly, I told him. "I've seen enough of white women's freedom to know that all women have masters. Look at Anne Bankhead, the master's granddaughter. She can't get free of her husband. He beats her. My mama and grandmama had more freedom than that. And they're nigra."

He sighed. "There's a difference, Harriet, in being a slave and being a free white woman."

I raised my eyes, waiting for him to explain it to me. He went on. "True, white women are subject to their husbands' whims. They can't own property. They can't vote or be part of the political process or even handle their own money. . . ." He stopped, still scowling. I was smiling.

"Very well. You've made your point. At my expense.

You're quite astute, Harriet. I like that. But you should know that the white world has restrictions. I don't deny that. What we all must learn is that we never gain any benefit without suffering losses. The gain you make is freedom. But it has a price. What is important is that you've made your choice. Do you understand?"

"I think so, sir."

"Your mother and grandmother made the best of the world they were given. Perhaps, in some ways, they were less restricted than some white women. *But their world was not of their making.* They simply took what was given to them and made the best of it. Do you understand the difference?"

I nodded.

"You made a double choice, Harriet. To be free. And to pass as white. There will be a price to be paid for both."

His gentle words reached far into me and made me shudder. I bowed my head.

"If you have serious doubts, Harriet, tell them to me now."

I bit my lower lip to keep the tears from my eyes. "No, sir," I whispered.

He nodded, but he was wise enough to know I felt more than I was letting on. "In Washington City it may be painful for you to see your own people and not be able to reach out to them as one of them. When you see them in poverty or bondage. Or even free but persecuted. Will you be able to bear it, without giving yourself away?"

"I don't know, sir."

"There is a way. I will help you."

"How?"

"As a white woman you may, at times, be able to ease their burden. Help those less fortunate. And certainly make the world better for your own children. I cannot help you with the losses you suffer for your gains, Harriet. No one can."

"Sir, you are kind to even think of them."

He blushed. "Enough of that. You insist on calling me sir. Well, perhaps it is best for now. You will need protection when you get to Washington City. A young woman alone . . ." He shook his head. "Not seemly. There will be too many questions. If you are in agreement, I shall tell people you are the daughter of an old college professor of mine. His name was Ethan Lackland. His wife's name was Prudence. They went down on a ship on a sea voyage to England six months ago."

He smiled, conjuring them up. "I was almost a son to them. They had a young daughter, Elizabeth, who died of pleurisy years ago. You may take her name, once you leave here. I will say he entrusted you to my care, that I am your guardian. We will tell my sister this also, so as not to burden her with the truth, which will be known only to us, Harriet. No one must know who you are. Or it will not go well for you."

"My grandma's name was Elizabeth," I said.

"Then in your mind it shall be your grandma's name."

I spoke my mind then. "The master said that lying is never good. He says once a person tells a lie they must tell another. And they no longer know the truth."

He nodded gravely. "I hold Mister Jefferson in the highest esteem. But do you think he is living the truth?"

I was struck speechless.

"He hates slavery and keeps slaves."

"He says slavery is a wolf America holds by the ears," I told him then, "and America can no longer hold onto it. And cannot let it go."

He sighed. "Ah, yes, I sense how torn he is by it. His slaves are the best cared for I have seen. But he has made compromises. As must we all. And oftimes that means lying."

Oh, I didn't want to hear such things about the master!

"I know you love him, Harriet," he said patiently. "I admire you for that. Yes, you will be inventing a life for yourself in the white world. Once you go down that mountain you will be Elizabeth Lackland. But half the people in this country invented themselves when they came to these shores. All were running from something."

He smiled at me again now. "We're going to take that wolf by the ears, Harriet. Both of us. We're going to give him a good shake and we're going to let him go."

I had never thought of matters the way he did. I was learning.

"Your beloved Thomas Jefferson invented the country itself when he wrote his declaration. He invented it as he went along."

Never had I heard such things.

"May I tell Mister Randolph this tea was beneficial to us both?"

"Yes, sir. But must you go?"

"Is there something more you would ask me?"

"Would you tell me about Washington City?"

One eyebrow went up. Truth to tell, I wanted to detain him. For by now I was determined I was in love with him.

I do not know what love is. Or what it is supposed to feel like. But I knew he was the center of the world for me now. And when he left, this place would be dark and cold.

He was chatting about Washington City. "We have many shops along Pennsylvania Avenue. We have bridges across the Potomac and steamboats that travel on the river. The stagecoaches go regularly to Fredericksburg and Baltimore and Philadelphia."

I was under his spell. I could see the city. I could conjure it up, built by his words.

"We have the Botanical Gardens and many churches and philosophical societies. President and Mrs. Monroe are well liked. Their table is richly furnished. But not the way it was when Mister Jefferson was President."

He smiled at me. I felt sure I would faint.

"Of course, we have been affected by the depression that grips the land. But not very badly. Land values have dropped, and some banks have failed. But the presence of the federal offices keeps things going. Why, in the navy yard alone we employ three hundred and eighty civilians. You must call me Thad, Harriet. That is my name."

His name! Of course! Oh, what a wonderful name!

"Thad Sandridge. For your own protection, mention it to no one."

I swore I wouldn't.

"Is there anything else about me you want to know?"

I asked him about the work he did then. He was flattered.

"The most outstanding thing I've done is draw up plans for a brick building in Washington City."

"Is it great? Like the master's university?"

"No, I fear not. It is substantial, though. And it has a degree of importance."

"Tell me why."

"The Fourteenth Congress met there."

"And that made it important?"

He laughed, showing his straight teeth. "You are most refreshing. It wasn't what Congress did there as much as the fact that they agreed to use the building. You see, the British burned parts of Washington City several years ago."

I told him I knew. I told him the master sold off almost all his books to the Library of Congress to replace the ones they lost.

"I must never forget how educated you are," he said quietly. "Well, after the British burned parts of the capital, there were many people who wanted to move the government out of Washington City. I was asked, by a group of far-thinking men, to draw up plans for a building in which Congress could meet. They thought if they could erect such a building it would be a symbol of the future of the city."

"And was it?"

"There is no more talk about the government moving out," he said.

I had never known a man in my life, except the master, who had done anything really important. For the first time it came to me that Thomas Jefferson need not be my whole world.

"And now I must take my leave," he said.

He came toward me, bowed, and leaned to kiss my hand again. I went hot and then cold as I viewed the top of his curly head. I longed to reach out and touch the curls. He straightened up. His shoulders, beneath the well-cut frock coat were so broad. The ruffles at his throat so white. His chin so strong. His cheekbones so bold.

I did not want him to go.

"Until we meet again, Harriet. I shall write to you." His eyes burned into me. I felt dizzy. The room was whirling around me. The closeness of him, the strength, the masculinity, made me come alive in ways I had never known.

"May I be so favored that you will return my letters?" he asked.

"Yes, sir. I will await them."

"Call me Thad. Once before I go."

"Thad," I said.

"And before you leave here, Harriet, do one favor for me."

"Anything, sir."

171

He frowned. "No, don't say that. Don't be too eager. Hold back some part of yourself, always. It is done that way in the white world."

He saw confusion in my eyes. "There is so much for you to learn. Yet I look forward to the task. But back to the favor I ask. Once, before you leave, call him Mister Jefferson. Do it for me."

This man was going to break my heart, surely. "Such freedom," I said. "I cannot."

"You must start to practice freedom, Harriet."

I told him it would upset the natural balance of things, me talking to the master like that.

"When Mister Jefferson wrote his declaration, he upset the natural balance of things," he said.

I told him then that I did not know if I would ever have the wits to survive in the white world. "I think it breaks one's heart," I said, "if one is not careful."

"It breaks one's heart every day, Harriet. Even if one is careful."

Had he had his heart broken, then, I asked. Indeed, he said, many times. Oh, those eyes! When he looked at me I saw it was true. I saw swirling depths of sadness in those eyes. But he was so exciting! Oh, then I realized he still held my hand. I blushed, and he released it.

"But you survived," I told him.

"I will teach you to survive," he promised me. Then he smiled. "Pray this year goes quickly," he said. And then he leaned forward and kissed my forehead. I was so startled. But it was more like a blessing than a kiss. "Until we meet again," he said.

172

Then he turned on his heel and left. I watched him stride through the dining room. And it was filled with his presence after he was gone. I felt heady, as alive and besotted as the servants get on Christmas Day with rum.

My hand tingled where he had kissed it. Oh, I didn't want him to leave! I wanted to go with him!

And that is how I met the man I intend someday to marry.

October 1821

Leaving. I am leaving. There've been days these last few months when I awoke in the middle of the night thinking on it. And the thought would hang there in front of my mind. Just like a bright star somebody pinned up there in the heavens above Monticello.

Leaving this place. Forever.

Going into a white world. No more nigra servant. What is it like to be a white lady? Suppose I can't do it? Suppose people find out? How will I ever learn to stop being me — Harriet Hemings from Monticello, whose mama is Sally Hemings?

And then I would think of Thad, so handsome, so kind, talking to me about Washington City and kissing my hand. And I can't wait for my twenty-first birthday.

But Thad is gone now, and though I can conjure him up at night, when I'm lying in bed, or in daytime, when I'm up and about this place, it's different. The thought of leaving works its way into me. It's like a heavy stone I have to swallow, bit by bit. And swallow and chew on. And then it lays there like a solid lump inside me, dragging me down. So I'm almost ready to go to Mammy Ursula and ask her for a preparation of mustard seed to help my digestion.

Then a letter comes from Thad. Right from Washington City! To me, Harriet Hemings, here at Monticello.

When they bring the mail up the mountain from the post office in Charlottesville, it goes directly to the master.

One day, a fortnight after Thad left, the master summoned me and handed me a letter. "From Washington City, Harriet," he said.

I curtsied. "Yes, Master."

He was holding the letter in his hand, and he had on his face that bemused smile of his. Oh, what shall I tell him if he asks, I thought. My hands began to sweat as I fussed with my apron. But, thank the Lord, Mister Randolph had already explained things to him.

The master held the letter out to me. "Mister Randolph tells me you wish to become betrothed, Harriet," he said.

I lowered my eyes most decorously and said, yes, Master, with your permission.

"I should scold you for being a rogue and not telling me you had made the acquaintance of a fine gentleman while he was visiting recently," he said.

Did I dare look at his face? Yes, I did. The blue eyes were kind. "My son-in-law seems to have taken you under his wing. He assures me everything is being arranged with the utmost propriety. Indeed, Harriet, I am most gratified. Mister Sandridge embodies the qualities I most admire."

"The cucumbers and watermelons are ready for picking, Master."

He smiled. "Thank you, Harriet. I shall inform Mister Bacon that you will be leaving when your time comes, and your betrothal has been arranged on the outside."

"Oh, thank you, Master!"

"I shall keep your secret, Harriet. It would not be good to expose your plans in the white world to anyone. Henceforth, the letters from Mr. Sandridge will be delivered to you only by me. Letters give us great pleasure, Harriet. In their contents are those truths, which, though not doubted, we love to hear repeated. They serve as gleams of light, to cheer a dreary scene where envy, hatred, malice, revenge, and all the worse passions of men are marshalled to make one another as miserable as possible."

And so it was that Thomas Jefferson gave his permission for my betrothal.

I escaped the house with my letter. I ran into the orchards to read and savor it alone. I read it over and over again. I admired Thad's penmanship. I smiled in delight over the things he is doing in Washington City. And then I held the parchment close to me. I put it inside my chemise, close to my heart.

November 1821

Those moments when I receive Thad's letters, are, as the master said, as gleams of light to cheer a dreary scene.

But in between times, after I send my reply off to Thad and await his next letter, I think that I've become daft just to think of leaving this place. All Thad speaks of in Washington City seems so far away. Like a dream.

Now, as I write this, I have not heard from Thad for a month. And I am starting to ponder how twenty years of living on this place has been wiped out overnight.

And every day as I make my way around, the lawns and trees I know so well seem to argue with me.

Oh, this idea of freedom has grabbed onto me like a tick and is seeping into my blood. And I know it will grow inside me, like a baby I got on the wrong side of the blanket.

And I will go when my time comes. I know that as sure as I know the movements of the seven-day clock in the entranceway. But I mark here that sometimes at night, when everyone is asleep, I take myself out of bed and wander the halls and let my bare feet feel the cold floorboards in the downstairs rooms. Like a spirit I walk. Once I went and stood on the south terrace when it was wet with rain and looked out over the mountains.

Once, at dawn, before the household stirred, I watched the mist over the Blue Ridge. The morning was just commencing, and it was beautiful. The birds were waking up and going about their morning business. And I felt as if the whole place were mine. The mountains went on forever, getting mixed up with the sky. And then the sun came through the mist and I just looked and looked, printing the scene on my mind forever.

April 1822

I have been very remiss about writing in my journal. The year has gone so quickly. I am so busy I have scant time to mark here the happenings, and I must catch up.

I have tried to keep myself apart from what has gone on here all year. I have tried to hold myself away and not get caught up in things. But it is almost impossible.

I feel so alone sometimes. I no longer feel part of this place. Each time a letter comes from Thad, I get more drawn into his world. But I must still live here.

I have had some very bad dreams lately. They frighten me. I dream I am on the streets of Washington City, and though I do not know what the city looks like, I do know I am lost. I cannot find Thad. And then I come upon Mammy Ursula's cabin. I do not know the people on the front porch. But they shake their heads at me and tell me Mammy has died. That I broke her heart by passing into the white world. That I killed her.

Then I awake with a start, and I am sweating and frightened.

· · · · ·

All through the fall of last year and the ploughing, I stayed indoors and worked on my studies. Martha Randolph herself praised me for applying myself so diligently. I did not tell her it was because I could not bear to see them ploughing under the earth for the last time.

She was so pleased with me that she showed me an old letter her father had written to her. The year was 1783, a year after her mother died. And in it was a schedule he gave her for studying.

"There was scarcely a moment to enjoy a meal," Martha said. But she glowed with pride, remembering.

The master had given me no such schedule, I reminded myself. And doubtless this is why Martha showed me the letter.

The master knows I prepare myself to leave this place. But he barely speaks to me except to say something about the joy of receiving letters whenever Thad writes to me. Perhaps I am not really his daughter, then.

Oh, how I torment myself with such thoughts!

In November the master told us that less than an acre of pumpkins have fed nine horses at Shadwell, one of his other plantations, for five weeks. "As well as a gallon and a half of corn a day would have done," he boasted.

I find myself clutching such knowledge to my heart. And now, when I lie awake in bed at night, afraid to go back to sleep after that dream of being lost in Washington City, I conjure up all the bits and pieces of information I have inside me about this place.

The number of cattle to be kept on a farm must be

in proportion to the food furnished by the farm.

One half ounce of powdered brimstone will instantly extinguish a chimney fire. But you must throw it directly on the burning coals in the hearth.

It takes two pounds of washed Merino wool to make a yard of cloth. A quarter of a cord of wood a day will keep one fire and will do for heating five kettles.

Young hogs require a bushel of corn a month for four months in their first winter.

A sheep requires one fifth the food of a cow.

At shearing time you must mark the age of your sheep for the first three years by a nick, each year, in the right ear. But on the fourth and fifth years you must nick the left ear. And on the sixth year you must crop the left ear and fatten them for mutton.

A plough horse gets an allowance of ten barrels of corn a year.

When I go to Washington City, what use will this knowledge be to me? When I am the wife of Thad, what will I do with it?

I have learned these matters as other children learn their sums.

What good will this do me when I teach orphans?

When May comes in Washington City, will I think how a gallon of lamp oil, which costs a dollar and twenty-five cents, will have lighted Master Jefferson's chamber brightly for twenty-five nights of the month? For six hours each night? Costing the master only five cents a night?

Will I ever be able to light an oil lamp without thinking on this?

They butchered the most hogs ever last December

here. The master said it would be a bad winter, and it was. The deepest snow we ever had fell this past Christmas. It was three feet.

I ran outside and played in it with the master's young grandchildren.

At Christmas we had the great tree in the parlor again. I pricked my fingers so with needles, stringing the popcorn. But I did not mind. For I knew it would be for the last tree I would ever enjoy on this place.

They planted beets on March sixth of this year. Spinach on March twenty-fifth. By August twenty-sixth, when they sow the winter spinach, I will be gone.

But shall I ever forget that a hundred pounds of green pork makes eighty-eight pounds pickled? Or seventy-five pounds of bacon?

May 15, 1822

Today I almost had a fight with Martha.

We were in the parlor with all the doors open to make the place as airy as possible. The heat has come early this year. It is probably the last week of quiet we will have before the summer guests start arriving.

I was doing a French seam on a new chemise for myself. Everything was most agreeable until she opened her mouth.

"It's a shame your father never cared to do for you what the master is doing," she said.

"Ma'am?" I asked. My needle stopped.

She repeated what she had said. My heart started beating so loud in my chest I just knew she would hear it. So I put my hand there to quiet it. But it wouldn't quiet.

"My father?"

"Oh, I know your mama hasn't told you. And she

182

never will. Your father, as near as we can figure, is Peter Carr, the master's nephew. He spent numerous summers at Monticello years ago. My father spoiled and indulged him, because he is the son of my father's sister."

And then she shakes her head. "It was no way to repay my father for his kindnesses, mixing with the servant women and producing children in so irresponsible a fashion. But then, Peter Carr never was very responsible. I suppose that's why my father feels obligated to help Sally Hemings' children."

Well, by then my heart was racing like B'rer Rabbit being chased by B'rer Fox. Peter Carr! My hands were sweating. "Where is he now?" I asked.

"Oh, you know he is married with children and a law practice in Baltimore. He never comes here anymore."

Peter Carr. It came back to me then. My mama had said years ago that he owned Mama's sister Critta and had fathered her children. Had Mama lied to me? Had he fathered us?

No, no! It couldn't be! "Why are you telling me this?" I kept my voice plain and quiet.

"I thought you should know before you leave here, dear," she smiled at me indulgently.

I mark here that I stayed dignified. I started stitching my seam again. Of course, I said to myself, she is planting doubt in my mind about the master being my father. I decided to ask Beverly. It kept me from throwing myself at her and tearing her eyes out of her head. Beverly will know, I thought. I am sure of it.

May 17, 1822

It is two days later as I write this. I saw Beverly today for the first time in almost a fortnight. One might think I would see him every day. But this is such a big place and Beverly has been keeping to himself a lot lately.

I caught up with him on Mulberry Row just before going to the house for my noon meal after a morning of weaving.

"Beverly!" I called to him and he stopped and turned and smiled at me.

"Beverly!" I ran to him and flung my arms around him.

"Why are you so loving, sister?"

I stepped back. "Because you're smiling. I haven't seen you smile in such a long time."

"How are you doing, Miss Fine White Lady Harriet," he said. But it was not said in anger. It was more akin to amusement.

"Beverly, what are you up to?" I demanded.

"At least," he pretended to scowl, "when I go, I go nigra."

The earth moved under my feet. And surely the sun moved, too, in the bright sky. "You're going, Bev?"

He looked past me, not at me, up the hill to the house. "I'm thinking on it," he said gravely.

"Oh, Bev." I took a step closer. "When?"

"Not for a while yet."

I sensed something then. The silence was spooky. He was keeping something from me! "Not fair, Bev," I said. "I've told you all my secrets. You have to tell me when. You will tell me, won't, you, Bev? When you're leaving?"

He moved the earth with a bare toe. "Tell you," he said, "but not him."

"Oh, Bev!" I took a step back. "You'd leave without telling the master?" I felt tears gathering. Oh, how it would break the master's heart if Bev went that way!

"I don't want him to know," he said softly.

"But you've been so close all these years!"

"The years mean nothing," he says then. "If they did, I wouldn't be going now, would I?"

Men, I thought. How different their minds work. They cut everything down to simple and plain without the embroidery or the lacework on the edges.

"Don't do that to him, Bev. It will kill him."

He shrugged.

"You care about him. I know you do."

He said nothing and I went on. I got braver. "You can't expect him to send you to the university, Bev."

"I can if I think he's my father."

So there it was again, like a great dark cloud over both of us. And it will always be with us, I know. No matter where we go. Oh, why can't they give us the answers?

"Maybe he isn't our father, Bev. You ever thought of that?"

"No," he said.

"Well, what if he isn't?"

"Then who is?"

"Martha Randolph doesn't think he is. She's said things to me."

185

"What kind of things?" he asks. And his eyes are narrowed.

"She said our daddy is Peter Carr."

He spat into the dirt. "Bah! She tried to say the same thing to me a while back."

"You don't believe her?"

"No."

"Why?"

"Because," he says softly, "I already looked up the dates Peter Carr lived here."

My heart leapt inside me. Oh, that Beverly is a smart one, all right! Can't fool him. "When did Peter Carr live here?"

"Don't rightly recollect," he said stubbornly.

"Bev, are you still punishing me because I'm passing?" I asked coyly. "I thought we had all that settled."

He let his eyes pass over me. And there was such wisdom and sadness in them I wanted to cry. "Got the dates written down somewhere," he said. "Suppose I could find them. But then you'll only have more high-falutin' ideas, Harriet. You got enough of them already."

But he was not angry with me. Only a vast sadness seemed to come from him. "When you leaving, Harriet?" he asked. "You'll be twenty-one in another week."

So that was it. My time was getting close. He was feeling time pressing down on us both.

"I won't leave before you go, Bev," I said. "I want to be here when you go. I want to say a proper good-bye to you."

He nodded, somewhat mollified. "Finding those dates when Peter Carr lived here won't prove anything except that he isn't our father."

"Find them for me anyway, Bev. I want to know that."

He nodded, agreeing. Then, after a moment, he said something else. "My life is ruined," he said.

Oh, I couldn't stand his saying that! I begged him not to say such a thing! You'll be free soon, I reminded him. I told him he was young and strong and educated.

"Ruined," he said again. "We're better off if we go out into the world not knowing he's our father, Harriet. Then we won't expect so much."

"No," I said. "If I knew he was my father, it would keep me strong. So please get those dates for me, Bev! At least I'll know that Peter Carr isn't my father."

He lowered his head and said he would, that he could never refuse me anything. "That Martha Randolph just wanted to plant some bad voodoo in your head," he said then. "If Thomas Jefferson wasn't our daddy, why would she bother?"

I nodded. "You make a whole lot of sense sometimes, Bev," I said.

"Just sometimes?" He grinned at me, and things were good between us again.

"Tell the master that you're leaving," I begged.

"That," he said, "I can refuse you."

We walked for a while along Mulberry Row then. We spoke of other things, catching up on plantation news. And then he told me this: The night before I go, he said, I'll write out the dates Peter Carr lived

187

here and leave the paper under your pillow. When you find it, come there. And he gestured to the orchard below Mulberry Row. "I'll be waiting," he said. "To say good-bye."

When I leave this place, I will leave knowing many things. I will know that a hundred bushels of wheat make twenty barrels of flour, and that when artichokes are planted flush, the rows should be two feet apart.

I will know that you plant peas in June, and that a pound of salt is necessary for curing every ten pounds of pork for bacon.

But I do not know, nor do I think I will ever learn, how I am going to say good-bye to my brother.

I must write this down before I forget. I sought my mama out, directly after, in the wine cellar in the passageway underneath the house. I wanted to know how she felt about Beverly leaving.

In our conversation on Mulberry Row, Beverly had said he'd told mama he was leaving. And that he'd cautioned her not to tell the master.

Would mama abide by his wishes? Beverly had said yes, she would. I had to speak to her. I had to know, right now, what she was thinking. She was happy over my going, as happy as any mama could be under the circumstances. Would she be just as satisfied about Beverly?

Outside it was hot and bright, the air filled with the fragrance of jasmine and honeysuckle. But down under the house it was cool.

I found Mama sitting on an overturned barrel, sipping a cup of tea.

"What are you doing, Mama?"

Her head was turbaned, which meant she'd been working. The folds of her faded dress fell on bare feet. She looked tired. Her cup clinked in the saucer as she set it down. If I talk to her about Beverly leaving, I told myself, and see sadness in her eyes, I will know how she will really feel when I leave. She had not hinted anything of that to me. And this will be my way of knowing.

"I'm hiding," she said. And she smiled like a little girl.

"You?"

She has a very musical laugh. "Sometimes I do this. Especially after a morning of work. We were sorting out linen all morning, trying to decide if there will be enough for all the beds when the summer guests arrive. As usual, there won't be."

She stretched her arms over her head. Then she folded them in her white-aproned lap and looked at me.

"What are *you* doing?"

"Looking for you."

"Aren't you supposed to be with Martha, reading French? Or learning some fancy needlework?"

"Martha has a headache this afternoon."

My mama sighed. "I came down here to select the wine for dinner. Francis is coming today with his Mary Elizabeth."

"When are they getting married?"

Mama smiled. "November. My, I can't believe that boy is old enough to be married. I can close my eyes and still see his mama, the way she looked when I was sent to France with her to meet the master."

Francis Eppes is the son of Maria, the master's other daughter, who died. She and my mama and Martha had been girls together.

"He's twenty, Mama," I reminded her.

"So he is."

"Martha says he's a rowdy."

"Well, Martha ought to cast an eye on her own boys. They run us ragged when they're here, and when they're in school in Charlottesville they run Reverend Hatch ragged."

My mama stretched again, like Cromwell the cat. "Master told me he's going to give Poplar Forest and a thousand acres of land to Francis when he marries."

I nodded, thinking of Beverly. The master could do so much for his grandson, yet nothing for Beverly, who truly believed the master was his father.

"We're having rice soup, *boeuf a la mode* and *chartreuse* for supper."

"What's *chartreuse?*" I asked.

She lowered her eyelids. "Vegetable mold. We're also having wine jelly and cutlets of mutton and rabbit in mustard sauce and an Italian dish the master loved to have when he was in the President's house. It's called macaroni. Oh, and we're having ice cream in pastry balls. I recollect when I was a child in Paris how my brother James could make pastry! What an education the master gave him! What a masterful cook James was!"

I sighed. If she started remembering James or talking of the old days in Paris, I would never be able to talk to her about Beverly. Sometimes I just know my mama uses her memories as a shield. Nobody has such memories, of course. We children are always silenced before them.

"James," she sighed. "He died the year you were born, you know."

"He killed himself," I said.

She did not want to hear, however, how her Jamie had never been able to live out the freedom the master had given him one Christmas Day so long ago, in 1796, after they had all returned from Paris.

She shook her head with pure abandon. "Wild and crazy he was, that Jamie. But, oh, I loved him so!"

I allowed her her few moments of memories. But I wanted to speak of Beverly.

"Beverly is leaving, Mama. He told me so today."

She raised her eyes to the ceiling. "Let's see, what else are we having for supper? Fruits, nuts, and plenty of wine. I know he's leaving. He told me."

"Doesn't it hurt you, Mama?"

"Hurt me that he's taking his freedom? I *got* that boy his freedom before he was born, child. Just like I got yours for you!"

"Doesn't it hurt you that the master is doing so much for his grandson? South Carolina College wasn't good enough for Francis. The master had to bring him home to study law."

Her eyes were inscrutable. "His father, John Eppes,

couldn't afford to keep Francis any longer at college," she said quietly. "Mister Eppes is in poor health and has financial troubles. He can do no more for his son. And you forget that young Francis is the only living child of the master's beloved dead daughter, Maria. Would you have Thomas Jefferson throw the boy out into the street?"

Oh, she had all the arguments. One melted like a beeswax candle before her sharp retorts! No, I thought to myself. But that's what he's doing to your son, turning him out into the streets.

I looked for signs of sorrow in her face for Beverly. But I found none. And it enraged me. "I know you got us all our freedom a long time ago, Mama," I said. "But aren't you sad over Beverly?"

She picked up the cup that she had set aside on the brick floor. She sipped the tea, which must be cold by now. She stared into the cup and ran her delicate fingers around its rim.

"Go study your French," she said.

"I know my French."

"You didn't know what *chartreuse* is."

"Mama!" I wanted to scream at her, but it would do me no good. I knew that. I love her, but it is so wearying sometimes. She lives in two worlds. She has her private world that has to do with memories of France. It is a world of dreams that she holds onto. We children are the world she sees when she wakes up.

The way she says "we've having," when she talks about the meal. As if she will be there at the master's table when Francis and his betrothed come. She won't be. She is not allowed at the table. That is where the line is drawn between her dream world and the real one.

I don't understand how she can live two lives like this. I don't understand how she can keep them separate. But I think she knows she must or she will go mad.

"Beverly wanted to go to the university so bad, Mama," I said. "He wanted the master to send him."

"Yes, and I wanted to be the Queen of France when I lived in Paris. You children got to know your place!" She came alive then. She hissed the words at me.

"You've had so much here! More than anybody on this place! The master has been so gentle with all of you! He's taken from Beverly what he's taken from no one else. I've seen it with my own eyes. Yes, Beverly's leaving. It's time. It's best he goes. If he stays, he'll ruin things for himself with the master. Or do something terrible and end up on the end of a rope. And not even the great Thomas Jefferson will be able to save him."

"Mama," I said.

"He's like my brother James," she said then. "So handsome. Just like James was. When he walks through this place, I see James all over again. He has that same proud walk. He even holds his head the same arrogant way. So full of himself. Such moods. You think I don't see it? You think I don't have fears?"

I said nothing. She went on.

"You think I don't feel? You think he isn't taking

part of my heart with him? Children do that, even in the best of circumstances. And these circumstances are far from the best, Harriet, good as they be. I look in Beverly's eyes and see my own heart there. Torn to pieces."

And she placed her hand on her heart.

"Mama," I said, "I'm sorry."

She got up then, and picked up a cloth and started dusting off some wine bottles. She held a bottle to the light as she dusted, examining it, making it gleam.

"Mama," I said, "James couldn't live with the freedom the master gave him as a free nigra. You think Beverly will be able to?"

She didn't look at me. She just kept polishing that old bottle of wine, smiling secretly to herself as she did so. "Don't you worry 'bout Beverly being able to live with the freedom," she said to me. "James got all kinds of fancy notions living in Paris. Virginia isn't Paris. You children been schooled here by me. And Mammy Ursula. You children got your feet firmly planted in the ground. Now, go study your French."

That was all. She would discuss no more. I had no chance to even broach the subject of Beverly running off without telling the master. Or find out if she would abide with Beverly's wishes that she keep his secret.

But worse than anything, I had seen no real anguish in her heart because her son had made his decision to leave. Yes, she'd said he was taking part of her heart with him. But that had seemed more like anger than anything.

So how then, would she feel about my going? That was the trouble with my mama, I decided. Always she

194

was inscrutable. Always she hid her true feelings. She was so good at it that I worried, lest she did such a good job of hiding them away that she might not be able, when the time came, to find those feelings again and bring them out into the sunlight.

That same day
May 17, 1822

Sometimes I lose the days as I write in my journal.

The master said he did the same thing with his Farm Book. Once, long before he gave me this journal, he showed me his Farm Book. "Sometimes I neglect to record some days," he told me. "That is why I am so gratified when you remind me to make notations."

Who will remind him after I leave?

Right after I left Mama in the cellar that day, I went to find Mammy Ursula. It was late afternoon. The drone of insects was like thoughts buzzing in my head. Everyone was in the fields. Only some half-naked nigra children played outside the servants' cabins. Then a thought took hold of me.

Super-ann-u-a-ted, I thought. I hadn't recollected that for months, but I did as I approached Mammy's cabin.

It was from a note made in the master's Farm Book. It was written under "*labourers.*"

"*Build the Negro houses near together that the fewer nurses may serve and that the children may be more easily attended to by the super-ann-u-a-ted women,*" it said.

I asked Beverly what it meant. I could never ask the master. When I am with him, when he allows me in his presence, I don't ask him questions. I just listen and let him lead the conversation like he would lead a horse.

Well, Beverly didn't know what super-ann-u-a-ted meant, either.

"Find out," I told him.

"How?"

"I don't know. Ask Mr. Oglesby."

But he never did. He forgot, I suppose. And so did I. Until that moment when I came near to Mammy's cabin and realized they were all built near together. I should have asked my mama, I thought. She's close to the master. She would know. She may even be super-ann-u-a-ted, for all I know.

Mammy was weaving a basket on the wooden porch of her cabin. Two children played at her feet. Her hands moved quickly. I think she could probably weave a basket blind if she had to.

I sat down on the step of the porch. She was humming. One of those little babies was lying curled up in a piece of quilt, near to sleeping, and the other one didn't look far from it, either. The humming came from low in her throat, sad and old. It seemed part of the rhythm of her weaving.

"So what have you got to tell me," she asks.

"Beverly's leaving, Mammy."

"So he finally decided to sprout wings. Why the sad face? It's what you wanted. I sprinkled that boy myself with good voodoo, last time he wuz here. It's God's mercy for all my prayers."

"He isn't going to tell the master when he goes," I said.

"So. He's gonna stroll," she says. "Like Tom."

I said yes. And it will break the master's heart. But she only laughed. "You know what Masta say when Tom run? He say, 'Let the rogues get off if they can. I won't stop them.'"

Master Jefferson often called us rogues. But now it sounded like we were a bunch of stray horses he didn't mind losing. "I'm going soon, too, Mammy," I told her.

She stopped weaving. "When?"

"Soon after my birthday."

"Well, I know Masta knows you're goin'. All the peoples on this place knows how you been studyin' and learnin' so you'll be fit for the world out there."

She kept on weaving but smiled at me. And I saw then in her eyes that she knew. Or at least that she'd heard rumors that I was going to be passing.

I said nothing. I hadn't decided what to do when this moment came, between me and Mammy. But now that it arrived, I could not tell her I was passing. She asked me then where I was planning on going. And, oh, the pain of it became unbearable. Because I could not confide in Mammy for the first time in my life. Because words I wanted to say stuck in my throat.

Because I was cowardly and could not admit to her my decision to pass as white.

"I'm thinking on Washington City," I said.

She nodded her head slowly. "Thas a big place. Nigra girl could get lost there. Or in trouble."

"I'll have free papers," I told her. I lied to her. "Master will give me free papers. I . . . have things all arranged, Mammy. Don't worry."

She bent over her weaving. "So you've got things 'ranged," she said.

"I won't be in want, Mammy." Oh, how could I ease her mind? And then it came to me. "Master Randolph is helping me."

She made a low approving sound in her throat. "He's a good man."

We sat in silence for a while. And, oh, I felt so sorrowful. Because she had said once that I had to take my freedom, for every nigra woman who didn't have it. But if I passed, how could I do that?

"Will you make me a basket to take when I go?" I asked.

"What you want wif' a basket from old Mammy?"

"I'll put it on my arm when I go to market. You have to buy everything there. I'll put in it fine things I purchase."

"Where you gettin' money for fine things?"

"I'll be teaching school, Mammy." I could tell her that much. "That's arranged, too. Just like you teach these little children."

She nodded, asking no more. For a while she hummed to herself. "You make sure any chillens you teach know 'bout B'rer Rabbit and B'rer Fox."

199

Oh, I will, I told her. She promised to make me a fine basket. With a special mark in it to keep away witches. Because she'd heard witches were bad in Washington City.

"I'll want you to give me your cures, too, Mammy. I want to write them down before I leave."

She raised her eyes to look at me. "You'll write down my potions?"

"Yes."

"Your mama knows. To cure a headache, wormwood tea or laudanum, if it worsens. I don't believe in bleeding for colic. Powders of rhubarb and ipecac for dysentary. In Washington City they'll likely inn-oc-ulate for the smallpox. Mix rum, onions, and cornmeal for burns. Your mama knows."

"I want it from you, Mammy. All your secrets for poultices, salves, and remedies."

She laughed then. And I knew I'd made her happy. "You mean all my decoctions?"

"Yes, Mammy. All your decoctions."

"Chile, chile." She shook her head. "Ole Mammy will give them to you next time you visit. But you could ask your mama."

"I'm out of sorts with her. She acts like she doesn't care Beverly's leaving. All she talks about is that Francis Eppes is coming for supper with his Mary Elizabeth. They're to marry in November."

She nodded. "I birthed him. Took a long time for him to come. Almost killed the masta's little Maria."

"Well, I'm tired of hearing about him, Mammy," I told her irritably. "Mama doesn't even want to hear about Beverly leaving."

Her hands never stopped weaving. "She cares," she said.

"Well, she doesn't show it."

"Some peoples doan want to show it when they know certain things or care 'bout certain things," she said.

Her head was lowered, so I couldn't see her eyes.

But I knew what she was telling me.

She knew I was passing!

She knew!

Oh, Mammy! I wanted to throw my arms around her and beg her forgiveness. I wanted to tell her that yes, I had my reasons, but mostly I was doing it for the safety of my own self and for that of my children.

I wanted to tell her I would always be me. Harriet Hemings. A nigra. I was not passing because I was ashamed of being nigra. Or tired of it.

I wanted to tell her I was taking my freedom for every nigra woman who couldn't have hers. And she and Mama and Grandma Elizabeth and all of them here would always be part of me.

"Your mama's heart near to broke when Tom left," she was saying. "She doan wanna go through that agin. Sometimes peoples pretend ignorance 'cause they can't bear the pain of letting other peoples know they realize what's goin' on."

"I know, Mammy," I said softly. "And I suppose the people they're pretending for should just go along with the pretending. Because it's a comfort to those who pretend. Isn't it?"

She shook her head yes. "So it's lak your mama got

a poultice on her heart. Sometimes peoples gots to wear a poultice on their heart."

"A poultice?" I asked.

"Thas right. Cover the heart over. To protect it. Sometimes peoples doan want you to see their hurt."

I nodded.

"And sometimes," she said, "some peoples understand why other peoples have to do certain things. Even though nary a word 'bout it passes between them."

"Oh, do you think so, Mammy?"

"I knows it to be fact," she said, plain and certain.

I got up from the floor and put my arms around her. She hugged me. Tears came to my eyes, and I could see tears in her own eyes, too.

"Git off with you, girl. You're crushin' my basket."

I stood back. "Will my mama have to wear a poultice on her heart when I leave?"

She grunted then. "When you go, I expects I'll have to come up to the big house and treat her for distemper," she said.

I left then, with a promise to return and write down all her decoctions. "You know what a super-ann-u-a-ted woman is, Mammy?" I asked.

She shook her head. "Thas what you're gonna be in Washington?"

"No. Master said there were super-ann-u-a-ted women here on the plantation. Nigra women."

"That so? Well, he must know. Man that writes a declaration of independency like he done knows such things. You think he means you?"

"No, Mammy, I think it was you he was talking about."

She laughed. We laughed together. And I knew I was forgiven. If not altogether forgiven for passing, then for not telling her. Oh, I knew there would always be sorrow in her to think I was going out into the world as white. But there would be a sorrow a hundredfold more in me because I did not have the courage to tell her.

"Chile, chile, git off wif you."

But she was pleased, I could tell. When I get to Washington City, I'll ask Thad what super-ann-u-a-ted is, I thought. Thad will know. But I was sure the master was talking about Mammy Ursula.

July 13, 1822

Oh, I have so many anxieties. I stay awake nights, worrying. And there is so much pain because I cannot confide in those I love. Like Mammy Ursula, Thruston, and others.

I turned twenty-one in May. All my life I have waited to be twenty-one. Well, I've been that for two months now, and nothing has changed.

And then, on the thirteenth of July, I found the note from Beverly under my pillow as I was preparing for bed.

I felt the crispness of the paper.

Oh, Beverly, I thought. Oh. Tonight.

I drew the note out and read it. "*In 1791, 1792, and part of 1793, Peter Carr lived part of the time here and part at Spring Forest with his mother, who is the master's sister*," he wrote.

"*He left to practice law and returned for some time in*

1796. By 1798, when I was born, he was long gone and married and practicing law, sister of mine. I looked this up. It is true. Think what you will but I know he is not my father."

Oh, Beverly. My brother. So thorough in all you do. So exact. You are so good at figuring things. When you make your mark on a piece of paper or a piece of wood, you are always so certain, so right.

I sat alone holding the note for a while. I felt as lonely as a sparrow. Yes, I was happy Beverly had proved Peter Carr wasn't our father. But I felt so desolate. Because the presence of the note under my pillow meant Beverly was leaving.

Tonight.

As I write these words, I work by candlelight. A light rain falls outside, and there is nothing left in my heart. I have just returned from saying good-bye to my brother.

I cannot sleep, so I write. Surely I will die if I don't get the words down. The master said that writing in my journal would help me sometimes.

The master sleeps this very night in his room, not knowing that Beverly is gone. He may not know for several days. I promised Beverly I would not tell.

I pray my quill pen does not break under these words. Earlier tonight I lay on my bed, fully dressed and covered with a light blanket. Sleep was impossible. I lay listening to the sounds of the great house all around me. They are familiar sounds. I just stared into the dark in my small bedroom here on the third floor.

Surely my heart was thudding so loudly it would

wake the whole place up, I thought to myself. My eyes searched my room, finding familiar objects. My shawl was there on the back of a chair. And there was the old basket Mammy Ursula made for me. There were some of my books on a small table, and next to them was my embroidery sampler. Moonlight filtered in my window. Half an old moon was sashaying in and out of some torn and ragged clouds. And the leaves of the trees rustled with a wind that said, "I am important. I bring rain."

I could smell the rain in the air. I could feel the weight of the house around me, all the years and all the people I'd known here, all the voices and faces floating there above me in the dark.

Then I heard an old familiar hooty owl outside the window. I dared not sleep because I was waiting for the clock in the front hall to strike the hour.

That clock would wake the dead. Some visitors who have slept in this house and heard it at night thought a washtub was being banged. Others thought it was the signal for the uprising of Monticello's slaves. As if Monticello's slaves could ever rouse themselves enough to make an uprising. Look at me and Beverly. We have our freedom and weep for taking it.

I am going to miss that clock, I thought. And I felt the weight in my heart like the weights on the clock itself that fall through the openings in the floor to the cellar.

Just then it struck eleven. Each gong echoed in my bones. I got up and reached for my petticoat, which was at the end of the bed. I took my shawl off the back of the chair. I would go barefoot. I would find my way in the dark. I had no fear of that. I know that if I live to be a hundred, I will still be able to close my eyes and find my way in the dark in this house.

My real worry is that I will never be able to forget it.

Outside the wind was picking up and the moon still hadn't made up its mind whether it wanted to be in or out of those clouds. I ran across the lawn south of the house to the straight road that ran below, to Mulberry Row. I walked the soft dirt road, past the quiet cabins of the servants, whispering to shoo aside a stray chicken. A loose plantation dog came over, sniffing and wagging his tale. I patted him, and he went back to lie down.

From somewhere in a cabin, a baby cried. I heard its mama hush it. In the distance I heard a horse neighing in the stables. I passed the stone weaver's cottage, where I worked every morning, eerily empty now in the dark of night. Farm implements, stacks of wood, and raw iron for the nailery loomed at me like unearthly creatures from the sides of buildings.

I shivered in the wind. I wrapped my shawl tightly around me. I should have brought a candle or a lantern, but I could not risk being seen in the dark.

Suppose, I thought, I get to the orchard and he isn't there? Suppose he's left already? Between the stable and the washhouse I took a path that led down the slope to the vegetable gardens and orchards below. The vegetable garden has four terraces, and it is just below Mulberry Row. I and my brothers know all the secret paths on this place, and I was there in no time at all. I knew just how to let myself down over the stone dry wall that separated the gardens from the orchard. And I knew where Beverly would be — in the apple orchard.

I will always be able to close my eyes and see that part of the orchard again, so peaceful. The apple orchard. I love every tree. We've climbed them all, my brothers and I. I know the way each tree twists and bends and invites children into its branches.

He was there. Beneath his favorite. Waiting.

I heard and smelled the horse before I saw him. Then I saw the outline of the animal. And as I came closer, I saw that it was Nightwing.

Nightwing. Sired by the master's own Eagle! Beverly was taking him!

My brother stood next to the horse. He was leaning against the tree trunk, and he held the reins loosely in his hands.

"Bev!" I whispered.

"Why are you whispering, sister? No one's about."

I came upon him slowly. And I tell you it was spooky, seeing him standing there, trifling with the reins in his hands, all gussied up like one of the master's grandsons. Why, he even had lace at his throat. And buckles on his shoes. His breeches were fawn gray and the frock coat blue, as far as I could make out in that dark.

"Bev, you look beautiful."

Oh, he laughed, all right, the first I'd heard him laugh in months.

"You look like blood kin to the Randolphs," I said.

"I am."

When he said that, it shocked me, I can tell you. I walked across the night grass, all wet and soft beneath my bare feet. Nightwing recognized me and whinnied. I went up to the both of them and touched the horse's soft nose.

"Bev, you're taking Nightwing?"

"Nothing but the best for old Bev."

"You're stealing him."

His laugh was deep and throaty. "Stealing? He owes me, sister, after all the work I did for him all these years. He knows that, too. Nightwing is small payment."

I allowed that to be probably right. "Your clothes," I said.

He looked down at himself. "I look like a right fancy gentleman, don't I?"

"Where'd you get them?"

"Oh, here, there, and everywhere."

I thought of the clothes Mama was preparing for when I left, up in that secret room of hers. "Mama?" I asked.

He shrugged. "She said the way a person looks out there in the white world matters. And she didn't want me to look like a corn husk mattress. She wanted me to look like a featherbed."

"Well, you look like a featherbed, then," I told him. "You even have shoes, Bev. Real shoes."

"Thas right."

"You said good-bye to Mama, then?" I had to ask him, had to know.

"Sister," he said softly, "what do you think?"

I just nodded my head. We were running out of

things to say. And I wanted to say more. Because I knew that when I got finished, he would go. That he was waiting for me to finish so he could go.

He patted the left side of his breast then. "I even have papers," he said.

"What kind of papers?"

"Free papers. They say I'm free. He signed them when I was twenty-one. Was going to give them to me to take when I left. Mama gave them to me now."

I nodded, taking it all in. "So he freed you, then," I breathed.

"Sure he did. Kept his promise."

I felt even more sad then, thinking of the papers in his pocket that were signed by the master. Thomas Jefferson. His signature there, inside Bev's coat.

"You be sure and get those free papers when you leave," he told me. Then he stopped himself. "No. You won't need them. I forgot. You're gonna pass."

We fell silent for a minute. I asked him if he was going north. He said no. Where, then, I wanted to know.

He sighed. "Don't know yet. Just going."

Nightwing tossed his head and Bev quieted him. "I got the note with the dates Peter Carr lived here," I said.

"Good."

"Thank you for the note. You were right. He can't be our father."

He just nodded. I patted Nightwing again. There were a hundred things I wanted to say, but they were all stuck in one lump in my throat. I couldn't commence to say one of them.

He looked up at the sky then. "Good night for travel. Smells like rain."

I agreed it was.

"I'll have to be moving soon."

I agreed to that, too.

But he didn't move. Just sort of stomped his shoes in the grass and looked down at them. "I wanna tell you something, Harriet," he said then.

"Yes, Bev?"

He fussed with the reins in his hands, not looking at me. "I was in the library with Mama when she got those papers for me. 'Course, I been in there before, you know that. Lots of times. He always let me go in and use the books."

I waited, for I knew something important was coming, something that would probably tear my heart right out of me, more than standing there and saying good-bye to him was doing. If that was possible.

"Well," and he looks up but past me in the dark. Over my shoulder. "Well, everytime I go in there I look at his Farm Book. You know that book he keeps? Where he marks down when the spinach comes in and all about the harvest and the flowers and such?"

"I know, Bev. He showed it to me once."

"Well, I check it every chance I get," he said again.

"What for, Bev?"

"To see. How he marks us down. You know how he marks us down, Harriet?"

I couldn't make out his face in the dark, but I could hear the pain in his voice.

"No."

"On bread lists. On blanket lists. We're on those

211

lists, you and me. And Mad and Eston. With all his other slaves."

I said nothing, for I could think of nothing to say. And to tell the truth, the full force of what he was telling me didn't seep into my soul yet.

"We're on bread lists, Harriet! I saw it! Right below Mama! Right above Ursula and Joe and Anne and Dolly."

"Mama?" I asked. "She's on it, too?"

His laugh was low and very bitter and it frightened me. "Thas right, Harriet. Mama's there, too. Just like we're on the lists for the shirts he gave out, and the hats and the woolens."

"Mama?" I asked again.

"We're slaves to him, Harriet. Nothing more."

I would not accept that. I could not. I fought to make the right words come out of my mouth. Oh, God help me, I prayed, standing there. Give me the right words! "He keeps lists of everything, Bev," I said. "It's his way."

"We're on his slave list," he repeated. "He notes that he gave bread to us. And how much. You know how important he is. When he dies, people will see those lists. They'll see we were slaves. A hundred years from now that's all people will see of us, all they'll know."

"That's not true, Bev," I said.

"No?" And he looks at me all defiant like. "Then let me tell you something else, sister. Something Mama told me. There isn't one scrap of paper in that whole library of his. Or anywhere. Not one scrap of paper that says what Mama is to him. Nothing that connects her to him. Nothing that connects us to him. Except those lists in that Farm Book of his."

For a moment I couldn't reason. I stood there dumb like, as if he'd put a spell on me. I'd never thought about any of this — lists, scraps of paper. But I saw now for the first time what Beverly was trying to say to me. We'd lived our lives here, and they had been good. But where it counted, where men wrote things down in their golden books that told about family, we were not.

Not one scrap of paper, Bev had said. With all the thousands of words the man had written and all the hundreds of pieces of paper he had, not one with his name connected to ours. Except as our owner.

"Why are you telling me this now, Bev?" I asked.

"Have to," he said. "You should know. You should know how things are. Your head is too full of fancy notions, Harriet. This is the way it is with him. He doesn't want the world to know we're his."

"But are we his, Bev?"

"You still doubt that?"

"I don't know, Bev. Don't know."

"You know," he said. "That's the trouble with you. That's why I wanted to tell you this. Make it easier for you leaving."

I nodded. "I'm glad you told me, Bev."

He had turned and was struggling to get something out of his saddlebags. "Anyway, what about Mama? Even if we're not *his*, even if you want to have doubts about that, you don't have doubts about what Mama is to him. But even she's on those slave lists. And she told me he's ordered her to burn every letter he ever wrote to her, too."

"He did *that*?"

"Thas right, Harriet." Whatever he was struggling to get out of his saddlebags was out now. He held it in his hand, but I couldn't see for the dark.

"She has no letters from him?"

"I didn't say that. I said he ordered her to burn them. Whether she did or not, she didn't say. Here," and he thrust something at me in the dark.

"What is it?"

Whatever it was, it was wrapped in a gunny sack. I unwrapped it and felt the cool firmness of a bottle in my hands.

"Wine," he said. "From his cellar. What's left of what I used to ignite the balloon with. I'm taking one bottle with me and I give this to you. Keep it."

"Why?"

"Just because it's all I have to give you. Wanted to give you something. When you leave and get to wherever you're going, you can have a drink on Mr. Jefferson."

I clutched the bottle close to me. "I won't," I said. "I'll keep it forever."

He grunted. "Now come say good-bye to me and get back to the house before you're missed," he ordered.

Good-bye! But that would be forever. I would never see him again. My brother Bev, who had tormented me and been a friend to me all my life.

214

"I can't," I said.

"Sure you can." He took the wine from my hands and set it on the ground. Then he took my hands in his. "You're a proper lady, Harriet Hemings," he said. "You're peach brandy."

"Oh, Bev."

"Wherever you go, you'll be peach brandy. Something to be savored."

I was crying. "Come on, now." And he took my face in his hands and kissed both my cheeks. "You'll make that fancy gentleman of yours a fine wife."

My heart was breaking, surely.

"Will you remember what we had here?" he gestured to the orchard. "All this?"

"I can never forget, Bev. How could I?"

"You better forget. You better forget right fast, missy. And make a life for yourself out there."

I nodded and gulped then. "Oh, I will."

"And whenever you get to rememberin', you just think on that Farm Book of his. And how he lists us in it. And Mama. You think of Mama. You get to weeping in Washington City, you remember that. And you smile, girl. 'Cause you won't be on anybody's bread list anymore."

I nodded. "Thank you, Bev."

He hugged me then. I felt the buttons on the front of his frock coat bite into me, he hugged me so hard.

"I'll never see you again, Bev," I moaned.

"Shush," he said, "shush. Don't think on that. I know where you'll be." He released me.

"You mean, I will?"

"Didn't say that. I just said I know where you'll be. That's all I can say for now, Harriet. It has to be enough."

I nodded, wiped my face with my hands, and stood there like a fool while he mounted Nightwing. He moved the horse slowly from under the tree. I followed. He sat the horse well, and I thought for all the world how he looked just like the master up there on Nightwing.

"Take care, Harriet." He raised his hand. The moon came out from behind the clouds just then, and lightened the sky, and he and Nightwing were silhouetted against it.

I reached for his hand, felt it in mine as he leaned down. Then I heard his low, throaty laugh. "Not one scrap of paper, girl," he said, "you remember that when you get to crying."

And then his hand slipped out of mine, and he moved away on Nightwing, slowly at first, down the slope to the road below. I stood there watching him go, seeing him weave in and out of the trees in a graceful canter. Then they were down on the road, and he wheeled the horse around and stopped. For one minute. He held the reins taut, though Nightwing was fighting to go, and raised his hand again.

I waved. Then he put his heels into Nightwing's sides and was gone.

I stood there, still feeling his arms around me, still hearing his throaty laugh. My brother Bev. Gone.

I was alone in the orchard. I stooped and picked up the bottle of wine and wrapped it carefully in the burlap and started back up to the house.

Gone. I couldn't believe it. Tears came down my face as I found my way up the hill and across the road and up the lawns. But he was right. About everything. I know that now.

And, kneeling here writing in this book now, I know it. And I thank him for what he gave me tonight. All that business about the lists and no scrap of paper linking our name to the master's. Courage, that's what Bev gave me. That was his parting gift to me. Not the wine.

I will blow out my candle now and get into bed and think of him galloping down the mountain all alone. And though I still cry, I am not sad. For I know I will see him again someday. I have to think that. No scrap of paper, I will think. And I will keep right on thinking it.

The Middle of August 1822

I write in my journal now for the last time as Harriet Hemings of Monticello. I intend to take it with me. I am sure that in Thad's sister's very genteel and commodious house there will be a place of privacy for me to continue my story in this book and keep it private.

I will be Elizabeth Lackland then. A white woman. I tremble to think on it. Will people accept me that way? Will I make some slip of the tongue so people will know the truth? That I am part nigra? And embarrass Thad? And then what will I do, a slave woman out there in the world without free papers?

And having them would show I did not have faith in Thad.

Oh, I am so confused! It is just a month now since Beverly left. I think about him every day. I ponder on where he is and how he is faring.

I depart early tomorrow morning. I am all packed.

All the warm and soft clothing Mama made for me is in my portmanteau. So is the bottle of wine Beverly gave me. You would think I was a high-born lady, with all this frippery. Why, my garments look as if they were sewn by the most high-priced mantua maker.

I have two letters in my reticule, one from Mister Randolph and one from Thad.

Here is what the one from Thad says:

My dearest Harriet,

I was prevented writing to you last week by a bad head cold, the worst plague on earth in the summer. I long to see you. I hope this finds you well. I have made arrangements to meet you the morning after you arrive at Gordon's, which is eighteen miles from Mister Randolph's plantation of Edgehill. Mister Jefferson himself outlined the route. It is the one he always used to travel to Washington City.

I understand Adrian Petit, Mister Jefferson's faithful servant, will accompany you to Gordon's, where comfortable rooms await you. It is only a country tavern, but the victuals are substantial. There is a room also for Mister Petit, who is acting as Ethan Lackland's lawyer, delivering you to your guardian. I understand Mister Petit was a good friend of your mama's when she was in Paris years ago with Mister Jefferson.

The route, as Mister Jefferson mapped it out, goes like this: From Gordon's we go to Orange Courthouse. The roads get difficult there. Seven miles further we come to Adam's Mill and enter the flat country, which continues for forty-six miles. It is two

219

miles then to Downey's Ford, where we will find a
good place to ford the Rapidan. The second day we
will have to travel to Stevensburg, since there is no
tavern from Orange Courthouse until we arrive there.
People here know Mister Randolph. They will not
know us. We will not lodge at Stevensburg, because
Zimmerman's Tavern is an indifferent house. The
food is not very good. We will go five miles further
to Mr. Strode's in Culpeper County. It is a most
commodious inn. But Mister Jefferson often stayed
there while traveling to Washington City. So we must
be careful you are not recognized by people who may
have visited him at Monticello. The next day the only
tavern we will pass that sleeps people is Bronaugh's,
at Elkrun Church. So we will have to lodge there.
Upon leaving Bronaugh's, we leave the flat country
and engage in a very hilly terrain. We will dine and
lodge the next evening at Brown's Tavern, a poor
place but obliging. It is eighteen miles from Brown's
to Fairfax Courthouse, the next day, and we shall
stay at Col. Wren's Tavern. It is very decent and
run by respectable people. The Georgetown Ferry is
six miles down the road, and we will take that the
next morning and be within miles of Washington
City.

My sister Jane will be traveling with me to meet
you and accompany us back to Washington City. I
hope the trip will not inconvenience you in any way.
We may have to get out of the carriage in several
places on the Alexandria Road between Fairfax
Courthouse and Col. Wren's, but that is the only
difficulty we will encounter.

Your rooms and meals at Gordon's have been charged to my account. I have told Jane that in the six months since the Lacklands were lost at sea, you were lodging with an elderly and infirm aunt in Charlottesville. Jane is anxious to take you under her wing and will not pry. This is not lying, Harriet. When one takes the wolf by the ears, one must summon up all one's wits.

And remember, before you leave, do your best to upset the natural balance of things and call the man Mister Jefferson. I long to see you. Until we meet, I remain your humble servant,

Thad.

Another note came to me from Mister Randolph:

Dear Harriet,

I have been in correspondence with our mutual friend, Thad, and all is in readiness for your departure. From his end he has taken charge very capably, using a route of travel which Th. Jefferson has often taken to Washington City. I am truly sorry I cannot be there when you take your leave. I know how difficult this will be for you.

My father-in-law has cooperated in every respect with me in my plans. But then he always did excel in the art of silent complicity. I truly believe he is relieved that your happiness is ensured. He has not enquired further into details about your future. He trusts that I have chosen the best of all paths for you. And I think he is happy that someone took this responsibility away from him.

Again, let me say I am most distressed that I cannot get away from Richmond at this time. But perhaps it is best I am not there. This is not negligence on my part. It simply means the sooner you separate yourself from that place and all who remind you of it, you will be able to start a new life of your own, without rancorous passion tearing at your heart for Monticello and everyone on it.

My dear child, it has been most gratifying to me to be able to help you. You may, of course, contact me in Richmond if you ever find yourself in a dolorous situation. But I think you will not. I know you will make the most of your new life. I shall be rewarded, many times over, even though my resolution never passes the legislature about Virginia's slaves, knowing I contributed somewhat to your freedom.

Courage, Harriet. You are escaping the velvet trap. There are those of us who will never do so. Your enduring, if somewhat mad, friend,

Th. Mann Randolph.

This last week has been like a dream. One moment I am feverish with excitement, the next, baffled by the unknown, and the next, exasperated at my own fears. I must write here now how it was with those close to me when I said good-bye.

But first I must mark how the master did not find out for almost a week that Beverly had left. Mister Bacon wrote him a note, a week after Beverly's leaving. "Do you know that Beverly has been absent from the carpenter's shop for about a week?" the note said.

The master did not know. He was white with rage

when he found out. And he seldom shows anger. He spoke to no one but Mama for a whole week afterward. As for Mama, ever since Beverly left, she has been strangely quiet. She seems to be retreating inside herself more and more these days. And when she looks at me it is as if I am already gone, too. Oh, how I long to throw my arms around her, but I dare not for fear she will break. For it looks as if she's been able to dig out her true feelings, after all.

How can I leave now, I asked her, seeing how angry he is that Beverly is gone. Her amber eyes shone with a brilliance that resembles fever. "Don't you understand?" she asked. "It isn't the leaving as much as it is that Beverly never said good-bye."

Sometimes, in the last few weeks, I saw the master on one of the porticos, a solitary figure. He'd stand there with his hands clasped behind his back, looking out over the hills. Oh, how I wanted to go to him, to stand there and say, "I am still here. I am still with you."

But what good would it have done? For I am leaving now, too. He knows. Mama has told him. And surely Mister Randolph has told him. Why, the master made arrangements himself for Mister Petit to drive me away.

Not only that, he gave me fifty dollars. Fifty dollars! I have never had such money in my life. Mama came to my room earlier this evening to make sure I was packed properly and to give it to me.

Madison and Eston came with her.

The four of us sat in my little room, talking. Madison and Eston were so quiet. They did more listening than talking. I held their hands while Mama spoke. But first she made me put the money away securely in my reticule.

"Why didn't he give me the money himself?" I asked her.

She just shook her head.

"Is he angry?" I asked.

She said no, just sad.

"Why should he be sad now?" I asked.

Because of Beverly, she said.

"It's too late to be sad about Beverly," I told her. "Beverly wanted to go to the university. He could have arranged it somehow. Then Beverly wouldn't have left."

We won't talk about that now, she said. That isn't what I've come to talk about.

"Why didn't he summon me to say a proper good-bye himself?" I asked then. "Is it because of Beverly? Am I to be punished because my brother ran off? Shouldn't he say good-bye to me properly?"

He will tomorrow, Mama said. Now she wanted to know, was I going to continue acting like an insolent wench or was I going to behave?

Well, she knew I was going to behave. There were just some things I had to say first. And so, having said them, I sat down and commenced to behave.

"It's too painful for him," Mama said quietly. "Remember, it isn't his way to speak of painful things. He never did. Not all the years I've known him. His way is silence. He was taught, since childhood, that silence is better than attack."

I didn't attack him, I told her. I only want him to say a proper good-bye. To talk to me. He has in the past.

"Your leaving is an attack," she said in that same quiet tone. "Even though he permits it. Even though he allows you your freedom. You are leaving him. That is an attack."

Well, I wanted to die then, I can tell you. There are things too painful for me, I said. But I speak of them.

"There are things too painful for all of us," she said. "Do you think this is pleasing to me?"

I behaved then. I obliged her. I hadn't been thinking of her. Only myself. I'm sorry, Mama, I said. But I need him now. I love him. I need him to speak to me with his gentle voice. And to look at me with his blue eyes. Oh, Lordy, Mama, I need him to speak to me. What will I do if he doesn't tomorrow morning? What will I do?

"He will speak to you," she said. "I promise. Just as I promise you will be all right. You must listen to me now. Will you listen?"

I said I would.

"All my life, everything I did was for this moment," she said. "When you go tomorrow, you forget about him, about us. You get married. Whether it's to this Thad fellow or to somebody else, you get married and have a family. And raise them right."

Yes, Mama, I said.

"Only you should know. I haven't decided myself yet if there is such a thing as a family. If it can be done. There's a secret to it, and I don't know what it is, keeping a family together. All my life I wanted for you and your brothers. That we should be here together as a family. Yet I only came back with him from Paris because he promised me my children would someday be free. And all it means is the end of my family."

I saw her pain, her confusion. I got off the bed then, and knelt at her feet. I pulled Madison and Eston close to us. I held their hands as I spoke to her. As long as I go on with what you wanted, Mama, I said, it isn't the end of your family. We'll be free, my family and I. That isn't an end. That's a beginning.

She listened. She smiled. Then she touched my face. "You're all grown-up," she said. "You have more sense than I thought."

Then she sighed. "All we women do, nigra or white, is want families. Worse than wanting freedom. We're fools, all of us. Look at Martha Randolph. Half her children here, half there. Her husband, God knows where. Her daughter, Anne Bankhead, with a husband who beats her. Even white folk don't know how to make families work."

I kept silent.

"Well, anyhow, we do get some moments while the children are growing." And she reached out her arms and drew us all to her. "And we've had some good moments, haven't we, Harriet?"

Yes, Mama I said, we had some fine moments. The boys agreed with that. And she kissed me then.

"Don't pay mind to me. I'm just an old woman and

226

a little bit crazy. All mothers are. Being a mother makes you that way. You remember that someday when you're a mama and you feel crazy. Your mama said it was all right to feel that way once in a while. I don't know what else to tell you."

She got up.

You've told me everything I need to know, I said.

She walked to the door and stood there. She looked so frail. Her white turban framed her face. "I loved him," she said. "That's why I came back from Paris too. No sense lying. Didn't say it was right. Just saying I loved him."

It was the first time she had ever spoken of herself and the master to me. I held my breath. I saw my brothers' eyes go wide. We were thinking the same thing. Would she tell us more now? Would she say he was our father?

"Living with a man isn't easy," she said. "A woman has to do most of the giving. Give pieces of herself to the man, to the children, to everybody. Sometimes it seems there's nothing left of yourself to give. I got you children and he took care of you. That's all I wanted."

I felt something fall inside of me. No, she wasn't going to tell us. The way she said . . . I got you children. Not, he gave me children. Oh, why couldn't she tell us? I saw my brothers' faces fall.

"Don't think marriage will be perfect. Don't expect it. Just try," she said simply.

I said I would.

She nodded. "Know you will. Well, that's all I have

227

to say. I'll leave you to visit with your brothers. Don't stay up too late. You need your rest. Just one more thing."

I looked at her.

"Times get bad. Sooner or later, for everybody. Those times all you can do is just go on lighting the fire and keeping the family fed and keeping everybody around you from killing each other. There's more of those days than I like to tell you about. Seems like you're always losing. But you're not. You keep lighting the fire and feeding the children and stopping everybody around you from killing each other and you're winning. You understand?"

I told her yes.

She smiled. "I'll see you in the morning. We'll talk more then."

Yes, I said. In the morning.

She left. I visited with Madison and Eston. We talked in low voices of our past, of their future. We swore eternal love for each other. Madison gave me a figurine he'd carved in the carpenter's shop. Eston had written down a tune he'd composed. I could play it on the pianoforte in Washington City.

I had to push them from the room. They were falling asleep on the floor.

The day before all this happened, I paid my last visit to Mammy Ursula.

I'm going to tell her I'm passing, I said to myself. I can't bear not telling her with my own lips. But when I got to her cabin, she was all smiles. She gave me a lovely basket, with good voodoo woven into it.

"I want to tell you something, Mammy," I said. "I haven't been truthful with you."

But she shushed me. She smiled. Her eyes looked so old. "Mammy knows all she needs to know," she said. "Right now, Mammy has a poultice on her heart. Now doan you go messin' with that poultice."

She held my hands in her own. So I quieted. No, I wouldn't mess with her poultice.

"Mammy knows everythin' 'bout this place," she said. "I wuz here the night in January in the year of 1772 when the master come up the mountain wif his new bride. They left their carriage at Colonel Carter's in Blenheim. 'Cause it couldn't make it through eighteen inches of snow. They rode a horse up the mountain. The big house wuz bein' built. They lived in the small cottage at the end of the south terrace. We servants had gone to bed that night 'fore they got here. Wasn't 'spectin nobody to come up in all that snow. There wuz no fire lit, no candles burnin'. But I wuz here."

She sighed. "I'se part of this place. But you ain't. You, chile, is part of somethin' else. Somethin' new. Out there. Go. However you wants. For all of us."

I held onto her so I thought she would break. "Make sure," she said as I left, "that no hooty owl screeches on your left side when you set out. Or you must come back and start agin."

Oh, Mammy!

Thruston gave me phials of seeds. He gave me Indian pink and larkspur and Persian buttercup seeds. We stood on the south terrace last night, when the August sky was high and lit with stars. The air was like silk. You could swim through it. The night was alive with insects, and there was a spell in the air. All around me I felt the spirit of Monticello, in the trees dripping with lush leaves, the fragrance of Thruston's flower beds. Inside the house the master was playing the violin.

"Handel," Thruston said.

The music seemed part of the night. My feet were bare, and the floor of the portico sent a warmth through my body, part of me.

"You're doin' the right thing, Harriet," Thruston said.

I said I knew. I said what of you, Thruston.

He shrugged and smiled. "Be right here, talkin' to the flowers. You doan worry 'bout old Thruston. No matter what happens 'round here. Even if old mister dies. Even if I gets sold. I knows gardening. I knows music. I'm a fancy buck. I'm valuable."

I put my arms around him. Oh, I wanted to die. I wanted me and Thruston to die out there on the portico with the sound of the master's violin playing Handel. I wished we could both be buried in the soft grass next to his flower beds.

"You grow my seeds in Washington City," he said. "And when they bloom, think of old Thruston."

I'll keep them blooming forever, I told him.

But he knew better. He always did. He always knew

things before I did, real things. The way he always knew I should leave. And what would happen to me if I stayed.

"You just save the memory of old Thruston," he said. "That's enuf."

The Middle of August 1822

My heart is so full. I sit here in my featherbed in my room at Gordon's Tavern. I suppose I should call it an ordinary, which is plainer than an inn. But although plain, the victuals are very tasty, and when we supped downstairs, the fire was warm and the room most commodious. We are eighteen miles from Edgehill. Not once, along the way, did I hear a hooty owl screech on my left side as I set out on this journey. So I know no bad things will happen to us.

Mister Petit and I dined on rabbit stew. I had hot, spiced apple cider and Mister Petit had flip, a drink of hot, spiced wine whipped up with egg. We finished with sweet breads and tea.

I scarcely slept at all on my last night at Monticello. I just tossed and turned in my bed. Today I did nod off a bit in the carriage, despite the bumpy ride. And I did see some fine scenery along the way.

Mister Petit is a most agreeable traveling companion. In the carriage, he told me how it was years ago when the master sent him from Paris to London to fetch young Polly, as the master's youngest — Maria — was called then. She was eight and had to cross the Atlantic to see her papa. My own mama went with her.

"Polly and your mama were staying with John and Abigail Adams in London," he told me. "Poor child hadn't seen her father in such a long time. She and your mama had a fine time crossing the Atlantic, however. They were the only females on the ship and much spoiled by Captain Ramsey.

"But then, in London, I had to stay three weeks before the Adams and your own mama, who was only fifteen and a child herself, could convince Polly to get into a carriage and journey with me to Paris."

He told me about my mama as a girl in Paris. Then he read his newspaper and dozed off, and I slept myself.

Once we got to this inn, of course, I was no longer Harriet Hemings. I am now Elizabeth Lackland. Mr. Petit gave me all sorts of courage, insisting I could "pass" easily, dear man. He's going back to France soon. He says he misses it dearly. But he says he is most gratified to be chosen by the master to deliver me to Gordon's safely. Even as he delivered little Polly years ago, from London to Paris, to see her father.

The dining room where we supped was very crowded with ladies and gentlemen. And although it is only a country inn, they were dressed very properly. I even saw one woman in silks and flounces. I wore my new cloak and bonnet in honor of Mama. In an anteroom,

233

some gentlemen were playing billiards. And in a far corner, some men were having a card game. But everyone behaved most decorously. There was a man playing a fiddle, and I thought of Thruston. I was so busy looking about I could scarcely eat. But Mister Petit admonished me to do so, and so I did.

All the fuss and bother by those who served us made me uneasy. Mister Petit whispered that this was as good a time as any to get accustomed to it. Then, when we finished, he said he would linger a while and have a smoke. And a chambermaid came to usher me up to my rooms.

She was tall and rawboned. She had a younger woman with her who must have been her daughter. I think the daughter is half-witted, poor child, for she kept staring at me with her mouth open. Her mother spoke sharply to her several times, and I was reminded of Mama chiding me. And I did miss my mama so!

Under the mother's watchful eye, the daughter turned down my bed, fetched water in the pitcher, and hung up my clothing. The mother must have thought I was a fine lady because she insisted on attending me, helping me out of my clothes, and brushing my hair. I suppose that Thad arranged for all this, and so I behaved in a most amiable manner, although no one had ever done anything like this for me before.

It came to me, watching the woman, that she was of a poorer class than I had known any white woman to be. For all the servants at Monticello are nigra. Her clothes and those of her daughter were clean but shabby and mended. That surprised me.

I never considered that there were white folk in the world worse off than I.

She then sent her daughter for some warm milk with rum in it so I could sleep. As I got into bed, she asked if she could come and assist me in the morning. For I told her I was betrothed and my intended was coming with his sister to fetch me for the rest of the journey. Oh, she said, you must let me come up and help you dress. Your hair is so lovely. I would love to dress your hair.

Well, I've never worn my hair in anything but one long braid down my back. It never occurred to me that it is lovely. But I thought I would allow her to dress it, as she says. Perhaps I will look better then for Thad. I thanked her. Then her daughter came with the warm milk, and they left, and I bolted the door from the inside as Mr. Petit had told me to do. I will give them some coins in the morning.

I got back into the featherbed and took my journal and quill pen in hand. They think I am white. I deceived them. They never questioned but that I am a white lady traveling with her lawyer.

I am not a darkie to them. I am not "high yellow," as they call mulattos on the plantation. Or even a "bright mulatto," as we are oftimes referred to. I am white.

Oh, I am in such a fevered state. I have never been away from Monticello before. And now here I am in all my finery, with my baggage all around me in a lovely room in a featherbed with a chambermaid with a half-witted daughter who wants to dress my hair in the morning.

Is this how white ladies live? I can hear the laughter and music from downstairs, and it is a friendly sound. I feel so secure and lovely. But I must mark here in my journal, before I get too tired, how it was when I left this morning. I must not forget.

We were up with first light. Mama came to my room to advise me to wear the good chemise and the striped petticoat and the stays of deep green. And, although I never was one to feel that fine feathers make fine birds, I felt almost a proper lady in my new clothes.

I went to the underground kitchen, where Mama had prepared my breakfast. Outside, the sun was just peeping over the mountains, which were still blue-black. Birds twittered with morning sounds. The lawns were covered with a fine mist. I sat and ate my hominy and some ham and warm biscuits with fresh butter and hot coffee. Mama just had coffee. She sat saying nothing. I waited for her to talk, reminding myself that we had a whole delicious hour to ourselves.

And perhaps she would say something to me now, finally. About the master being my daddy. Perhaps she had waited until the last moment.

But then, when I was finishing my breakfast she smiled at me. "The carriage will be out front in ten minutes," she said.

Ten minutes? I was horrified. You said we had an hour, I told her. She only smiled and shook her head. "It's just as well," she said. "Long good-byes are no good."

I felt so wretched! She had done this to me on

purpose! She had robbed me of this last hour with her! Why?

I had no time to think why. She was hurrying me out of the kitchen and through the underground passage and through the house for the last time. I saw faces in a blur all around me. Aunt Bett was there and Aunt Nance, reaching for me. All kinds of people were there who weren't supposed to be, popping out from behind walls and doors.

Burwell was there. And Thruston. And Madison and Eston. But someone was missing. Who?

They all said how fine I looked. I was handed from one to the other to be kissed and admired. I said words I cannot remember. Then they were all gone, just voices behind me, wishing me well. And Mama had me by the arm again, and we were in the entranceway, and just then the seven-day clock chimed. Seven in the morning. But someone was missing.

It's an omen, I said to myself. I hope I don't hear a hooty owl screeching on my left side. In the entranceway, I could see out the long windows to the roundabout in front, where the master was standing with Mr. Petit. The carriage was there, too. They were standing by it.

I stopped dead in my tracks. I couldn't have gone through those front doors just then if one of the master's jackasses pulled me through. Mama's hominy had gone right to my bones, turning them to mush.

"You go now," Mama was whispering in my ear. And she gave me a little push. I stopped and turned to her. Aren't you coming with me, I asked.

She just stood there, a small figure with a shawl wrapped around her against the morning chill. She folded her arms across her bosom and shook her head no.

Mama please, I begged.

She shook her head again. "You go," she said. "I got you this far. The rest of the way you go alone. Go on."

But I couldn't.

She took a step forward. "Then I will tell you something to make you go. Beverly said I should tell you this when you leave."

Beverly? Yes, that's who was missing. Beverly. But he was gone. What was she saying about Beverly. I must clear my head and listen.

"He passed," she said. "Your brother went out into the world as a white man."

The words made no sense. I just stared at her.

"Don't you hear me?" she insisted. "He said he's doing this not because he *wants* to. But because, more than anything, he wants to learn and to make something of himself. And this is the only way he can do it."

I still just stared.

"He said," and my mama's voice was low and musical, the way it got when she was pleased, "he said he's found a way to go to a university."

Oh, Bev! And something fell inside me. Yes, I heard Mama's words and I saw the triumph in her eyes, but just for a moment there this news she was telling me to make me happy was not doing the job. Because all I could see was the pride in Bev's eyes. All I could hear was his chiding me for passing. And though it had hurt me at the time, I'd been so proud of Bev. For knowing what he was and holding to it.

Yes, I'd made the decision to pass. But Bev had held strong to what he believed in. And now I know I admired him for it. And in that part of one's mind where that small voice lives that's always mouthing the truth at us, even though we lie to ourselves, I knew Bev was doing right by not passing.

Now here was Mama throwing words at me to change all that.

"What's the matter, child?" Her eyes went wide. "Didn't you hear what my lips are saying?"

"I heard, Mama," I said dully.

"Then what ails you?"

"Oh, Mama, I don't know. I never thought Bev would do it, that's all."

"Do what?"

"Pass. It's one thing for me, being a woman and all. But Bev was so proud. He was so . . ." I reached for words.

"Arrogant," she said. "And stupid. He's come to his senses, that's what he's done. Think on it, Harriet! Think how bad he wanted to go to the university! Think that now he can walk into any university and sit down, proud, and learn."

"But not as a nigra, Mama," I said. "And that's what he wanted."

She stepped closer to me. Her amber eyes filled with passion. "We don't get what we want when we want it, Harriet. With our people, we have to go the long way around sometimes. Bev is doing it. Oh, child, I don't care how he's doing it. Point is, when he's done and he's out there making something of himself and for his children, *then* he can come out and say he's part nigra. And he will, child, he will. And so will his children. And he'll be so proud *because* he had to go the long way around, but got there just the same."

"Will he, Mama?" I asked.

" 'Course he will," she said softly. "And so will you someday. Don't you worry. Now," and she encircled me in her arms and brought her head close to mine. "You ever know your mama to promise you anything that didn't come true?"

Oh, I thought my heart would break when she said that! I shook my head, scarcely able to speak. And she held me then, close. And we stood there and rocked back and forth in each other's arms.

Oh, the unfairness of it all, I thought! That on this day, the day I took my freedom, which should have been the happiest day of my life, my heart was breaking. "Mama," I whispered.

"Don't say it, child. Don't."

"I can't leave you, Mama."

"Yes you can."

"I don't *want* to! It's not fair! It's not right!"

"But you can do it," she said. And she released me and stood back, holding my hands in her own. "You can do it because you're my daughter. Because today, when you leave here, when you ride down that mountain, you're taking part of me with you. The burden of being a mother is that we can't follow our children when they're grown and it's time for them to fly. All mothers know that burden, white or nigra. But we also know that our children take part of us with them. And you know what else we know, to lighten that burden?"

"No, Mama, what else?" And I wiped the tears from my face.

She picked up the corner of her apron and patted the tears away. "We know that the part of us they take with them is the best part. And those children will do things we never dreamed of doing. In our name."

"Oh, Mama!" I hugged her again.

"And you're taking that part of me that always wanted freedom," she said. "You're taking that freedom for me. And so is Beverly. And so did Tom. So I can be at peace now. After all these years. So you go now; go on."

We pulled apart again. "Oh, one more thing," she said. "Beverly wanted me to remind you, when you go, about that scrap of paper. Said he'd tell you about it when he left, but I should remind you again. What does he mean? What scrap of paper?"

I smiled through my tears. "It doesn't matter, Mama. Bev just knew I'd need to hear those words now."

"Well, you got 'em. So go, then." She smiled at me and I smiled back. And I remembered what Beverly had said about our names not being on one scrap of paper in the master's writings. There was nothing to link us to him as anything but slaves. A hundred years from now, they'll know of us only as slaves, he'd said.

No, Bev, I thought. They won't. Because now we'll both be able to do fine things. Then something else came to me, and I looked at Mama. "You won't let them say, when I go, that there never was a Harriet. Like some say about Tom."

"They won't say it," she promised. "Not while I live."

"Not about Bev, either."

She swore to me she would box the ears of the first person who let such words pass their lips.

"I wish I could say good-bye to Beverly. I wish he knew how he's helped me."

"He knows," she said. "And now you take yourself and go, child. Run! For me! For all of us! And don't you look back!"

"Mama?"

She was walking away, melting into the shadows in the house. "Go!" she hissed. "Go! People are waiting for you! There's no more I can do for you now!"

My eyes were so filled with tears I could scarcely see. But I walked out of those doors for the last time, proud. My heart was hammering inside me. It's like you're walking with me, Bev, I thought. Like you're beside me right now.

Had the last laugh on me, didn't you? Saving up that news about passing until this last moment. I felt strengthened, walking down that path. I was not alone. I never would be.

They'd all be with me in my new life, Mama and Beverly and Madison and Eston, Aunt Bett, Aunt Nance, Mammy Ursula, Thruston, and Burwell.

Then I was on the roundabout, stones under my feet. The carriage was the master's best one. The master's landau, four wheels, closed. The top could be opened for fresh air. Mr. Petit turned, saw me, and bowed.

I curtsied. All my baggage had been loaded on already. The morning sun was bright enough to hurt my eyes now. And there was the master, smiling at me. He came toward me.

"Well, Harriet, you do look a proper lady."

Behind me I could feel dozens of pairs of eyes watching me from inside the house. And dozens more from around the plantation.

I curtsied again for the master.

"You look very grown-up, Harriet."

"Thank you, Master."

"Did you get the money I gave your mother for you?"

"Yes, sir. It's safe, here in my reticule."

He looked around him, at the landscape, the sky. "It's a fine day for a trip. You'll do well under the protection of Mister Petit. I understand you are to be met by congenial and trustworthy friends at Gordon's Tavern. My son-in-law insists I should have no fears for your well-being."

"I'll be fine, Master. Mister Randolph arranged everything."

"I've told Mister Petit to be attentive to the roads, as they begin to be difficult to find once one leaves Orange Courthouse. But he has my written instructions for the trip. He'll hand them over to your friends at Gordon's."

"Thank you, sir."

He sighed. "So you are going, then." His voice softened, and he looked at me. No one but Mister Petit was near, and he was standing near the horses' heads, conversing with the driver. I could scarcely keep my voice from betraying my feelings.

"It is well that you go. There is nothing for you here

anymore. You are young and strong, and I have tried to see that you are well prepared."

I nodded. There was nothing I could do. The sound of the man's voice, the strength and presence that emanated from him, never failed to put a spell on me.

"So, Harriet," and he clasped his hands behind his back and raised himself a little on the toes of his boots. "What notation do I make in my Farm Book for today? What do you have to tell me? That the sky is very blue? The temperature likely to climb? Or that there will be a full moon tonight?"

I drew in my breath. "That Harriet Hemings left Monticello," I said. I said it plain and quiet.

He stopped smiling. The corners of his mouth turned down.

"Will you mark it in your book, Master?"

He nodded, looking at the ground. "Yes. I will mark it in my book, Harriet," he said. "And now, since you have made up your mind to pass into the white world, I give some advice, the same I once gave my daughters. If you ever find yourself in difficulty and doubt how to extricate yourself, do what is right and you will find it the easiest way of getting out of difficulty. When you marry, teach your children to be good, above all things. Because without that, we can be neither valued by others nor put any value on ourselves."

I nodded.

"And always be true, Harriet. No vice is so mean as the want of truth."

Truth. What was he saying? Why, then, did he not tell us the truth? Why did he allow me to leave without telling me he was my father? What about the lie I had to live for the rest of my days as white?

Oh, I was torn between hating him and loving him. Then he went on.

"And never indulge in anger. It only serves to torment us. There is enough torment in life. Do not waste your energies over things you can do nothing about. No distress the world brings upon us can equal that which we bring on ourselves. What more can I say to you?"

That you are my father! I wanted to scream it.

I said nothing. Tears came to my eyes. He took note of them.

"Come now. We are always equal to what we undertake with resolution. My father died when I was fourteen, and I was thrown on a wide world, among entire strangers, without friend or guardian to advise. The dangers are great, Harriet, but your safety must rest on yourself."

What was he telling me? That I must go out into the world now without my father? That I was leaving now the only man I'd ever looked upon as a father? That he was my father? Oh, Lordy, what was he telling me?

"If you always lean on your master, whomever you perceive that master to be, you will never be able to proceed without him. It is part of the American character, Harriet, to consider nothing as desperate. When I was in Europe, I saw shops for every want. It is not that way here. Here we've been remote from all aid. We were obliged to invent and to find means within ourselves. We do not lean on others."

His blue eyes were piercing. I nodded. He considered

me an American, then. Not an African.

"My expectations about you are high, Harriet. Be industrious. Think nothing insurmountable by resolution and application. And you will be all I wish you to be."

The natural balance of things, I was thinking. There I was, looking up into the face of the man who had always reminded me of God. I knew him to be less than perfect now. Beverly had told me how my name was not on one scrap of paper that would ever link me to him in the future except as a slave. And here he stood, saying such wonderful words to me.

The natural balance of things. Those were Thad's words. Upset the natural balance of things before you leave and call him mister, not master. Remember, he upset the natural balance of things when he wrote his declaration, Thad had said. He will understand.

"You are now a cultivated young woman, Harriet. I have done my best with you. You will make your mark on the world, and so will your children. Go now; you have a long trip ahead of you. I have given you all I can."

"Master." He had taken my arm to lead me to the carriage and I hesitated.

"All that I can," he repeated. He gazed down on me. "There is only so much I have it in my power to do," he said.

This was his way. Forcing kindness on people when he could not make things better. Using innocence as a weapon. Silence as a shield. And ruling by kindness. Well, it was time then for me to break his silence. And his shield. It was time for me to speak.

"I know that, Mister Jefferson," I said to him. "And I thank you for all you have done for me."

His gaze held mine for a moment and there, in those blue depths, I saw the shock and confusion, yes, even the hurt. His head went back a little, with my words, as if I had struck him. But, true to what he was, to what he always had been when attacked, he responded with courtesy. And innocence. And silence.

"Have a good trip, Harriet," he said.

Oh, inside me something was singing! I have done it, Thad, I told myself. I have called him Mister Jefferson! I have broken my bonds! I am free!

And so I left Monticello.

His arm guided my elbow and I held my head high as I stepped into the carriage. Mr. Petit was standing there by the door, smiling. The sun, warm on my shoulders already, shone down a blessing. Behind me, I felt the whole place alive with eyes and with good voodoo as those I loved watched discreetly from a distance. I felt, rather than saw, my own mother standing on the portico, watching. I could feel the energy, the love between us.

Once, I turned, before the carriage started to move, to look back. The house, the trees, the lawns, the slender figure of my mama standing there all filled my eyes and my soul to the brim.

I smiled and waved at Mama. She nodded and waved back. Mr. Petit was sitting across from me.

I heard the driver urge the horses to move.

The last thing I saw was the face of Thomas Jefferson through the window of the carriage. And there were tears in his eyes.

Tears! For me!

Oh! I saw them, I saw tears in those blue eyes, though he was smiling. Tears for me! I leaned back in the carriage. My heart seemed to stop. I felt such a mixture of joy and pain that I thought I would die. So he cried for me, then. He was crying even now. Oh, Lordy, I thought, Lordy. Tears for me.

I took those tears with me as we drove down the mountain on my way to being free.

248

*Glossary of Terms of the
Eighteenth and
Early Nineteenth Centuries*

chemise — a full-length garment worn by women. The
bottom half served as a slip and the top as a blouse,
and was usually trimmed with a ruffle around the
neck and three-quarter-length sleeves. It was made
out of muslin or cotton.

dandy — a man who takes exceptional care in his dress

flip — a drink made of hot spiced wine mixed with
eggs

mantua-maker — a dressmaker

ordinary — a tavern

petticoat — a skirt

stays — a woman's garment used to enhance the figure. Worn over the chemise, they laced up the front
and were held in place by whalebone.

victuals — food

doxie — a woman of loose morals

queue — a man's ponytail

249

reticule — similar to a pocketbook, made of fabric
sanctum sanctorum — Jefferson's name for his private
  quarters, from the Latin for "holy of holies"
caudle — a warm broth served to the sick
phial — a small glass bottle

Bibliography

I have done much reading on the American Revolution and the statesmen who founded this nation. But the books I found most helpful for this novel, the books I referred to again and again, are listed here with my eternal appreciation to the scholars who wrote them.

Adams, William Howard, *Jefferson's Monticello*, Abbeville Press, New York, 1983.

Baron, Robert C. (ed.), *The Garden and Farm Books of Thomas Jefferson*, Fulcrum, Inc., Golden, Colo., 1987.

Bear, James A. Jr. (ed.), *Jefferson at Monticello*, University Press of Virginia, Charlottesville, 1967.

Bear, James A. Jr., and Edwin Morris Bettes (eds.), *The Family Letters of Thomas Jefferson*, published for the Thomas Jefferson Memorial Foundation, Inc. by University Press of Virginia, Charlottesville. Reprinted by arrangement with the University of Missouri Press, 1966.

Boles, John B., *Black Southerners, 1619–1869*, University Press of Kentucky, Lexington, 1984.

Boorstin, Daniel J., *The Lost World of Thomas Jefferson*, Holt, Rinehart, New York, 1948.

Brodie, Fawn M., *Thomas Jefferson: An Intimate History*, W.W. Norton & Co., New York, 1974.

Brodie, Fawn M., "Thomas Jefferson's Unknown Grandchildren, A Study in Historical Silences," *American Heritage, The Magazine of History*, October 1976, pg. 28.

Koch, Adrienne, *Jefferson and Madison, the Great Collaboration*, Oxford University Press, New York, 1950.

Malone, Dumas, *Jefferson and His Time, The Sage of Monticello*, Little Brown & Co., Boston, 1981.

Mapp, Alf J. Jr., *Thomas Jefferson, A Strange Case of Mistaken Identity*, Madison Books, New York, 1987.

Teller, Walter, *Incidents in the Life of a Slave Girl, Linda Brent*, Harcourt Brace Jovanovich, San Diego, 1973.

About the Author

ANN RINALDI is a well-known YA writer with a strong interest in American history. Two of her previous historical novels, *Time Enough for Drums* and *The Last Silk Dress*, were ALA Best Books for Young Adults. Ms. Rinaldi credits her son's interest in history with sparking her own, and the two are avid participants in historical reenactments.

A prize-winning newspaper columnist with *The Trentonian* in New Jersey, Ann Rinaldi lives with her husband in Somerville. She is the mother of two and is now the proud grandmother of Michael.

point

Other books you will enjoy, about real kids like you!